Dream Invader

'A richly original and skilfully crafted story
which blends elements of fantasy and folklore
with moments of true horror.'
BISTO BOOK OF THE YEAR CITATION

'Gerard Whelan's dramatic novel is a spine-chiller'
SUNDAY INDEPENDENT

'well-paced plot'
SUNDAY TRIBUNE

'Gerard Whelan's vivid storytelling makes us believe
utterly in his people and in a world that includes
an ointment that induces visions, a stone that
makes you invisible, and a stuffed toy
that turns into a huge talking tiger.'
THE IRISH TIMES

Special Merit Award to The O'Brien Press
from Reading Association of Ireland
*'for exceptional care, skill and professionalism in
publishing, resulting in a consistently high standard in all
of the children's books published by The O'Brien Press'*

Gerard Whelan

was born in Enniscorthy, County Wexford, and has lived and worked in several European countries. He now lives in Dublin, where he works as a full-time father. This is his second book. His first, *The Guns of Easter*, tells the vivid story of young Jimmy Conway's involvement in the Easter Rising of 1916, and is also an award-winning book. The sequel, *A Winter of Spies*, takes the reader behind the scenes into the intricacies of the spy ring led by Michael Collins. This time Jimmy's young sister Sarah is the hero of the book.

THE GUNS OF EASTER

**winner of a Merit Award and
the Éilís Dillon Memorial Award at the**

BISTO BOOK OF THE YEAR AWARDS

A WINTER OF SPIES

The sequel to *The Guns of Easter*

Items should be returned on or before the last date shown below. Items not already requested by other borrowers may be renewed in person, in writing or by telephone. To renew, please quote the number on the barcode label. To renew online a PIN is required. This can be requested at your local library.
Renew online @ **www.dublincitypubliclibraries.ie**
Fines charged for overdue items will include postage incurred in recovery. Damage to or loss of items will be charged to the borrower. *Irish author*

Leabharlanna Poiblí Chathair Bhaile Átha Cliath
Dublin City Public Libraries

Dublin City
Baile Átha Cliath

Central Library, Henry Street,
An Lárleabharlann, Sráid Annraol
Tel: 8734333

Date Due	Date Due	Date Due

First published 1997 by The O'Brien Press Ltd.,
20 Victoria Road, Rathgar, Dublin 6, Ireland.
Tel. +353 1 4923333 Fax. +353 1 4922777
e-mail books@obrien.ie
Website http://www.obrien.ie
Reprinted 1998, 1999

British Library Cataloguing-in-publication Data
Whelan, Gerard
Dream Invader
1. Children's stories
I. Title
823.9'14 [J]

ISBN 0-86278-516-2

3 4 5 6 7 8 9 10
99 00 01 02 03 04 05

The O'Brien Press receives
assistance from

The Arts Council
An Chomhairle Ealaíon

Typesetting, layout, design: The O'Brien Press Ltd.
Cover separations: Lithoset Ltd., Dublin
Printing: Cox & Wyman Ltd.

CONTENTS

DEDICATION

This book is respectfully dedicated to my son Davy,
who tried to tell me about his nightmares;
and (slightly less respectfully) to my brother Seán,
who gave them to him

ACKNOWLEDGEMENTS

Declan Costelloe and his boys at Ballyroan school, County Laois,
helped test-drive an earlier version of this story. Thank you all.

PART ONE

WHAT SASKIA SAW

It was certainly the strangest thing that ever
happened to her. It changed her life forever.
Looking back on it afterwards, though,
what struck Saskia most was the very ordinary way
it started. It had, after all, involved her uncle Phil;
and anything that involved Phil
was ordinary by definition ...

SASKIA

She'd gone to the city to stay for a few weeks with her uncle and aunt. Her father, who was a painter, was going home to Holland to make arrangements for an exhibition of his work. Saskia's mother, who was Irish, was travelling with him. While they were there they planned to find a place to rent for a few months, and once it was found Saskia would join them. But in the meantime it was handiest for everyone if she stayed with Uncle Phil and Aunt Ruth.

Saskia didn't much like leaving her home on the wild west coast of Ireland, where she woke every morning to the sound of the ocean on the strand at the bottom of her long back garden. It would be nice to be in Holland again, of course, but she was very much in two minds about this visit to the city that came first. Saskia didn't think much of Dublin. She wasn't really comfortable with her uncle and aunt, either, because she never felt they were really comfortable with her.

Aunt Ruth was her mother's sister, but though the sisters were fond of each other they were very unalike. Ruth worked in an office, and liked the city, and had married an accountant. Not that there was anything wrong with Uncle Phil, he was just a bit ... well, dull.

Saskia's mother, though born there, hadn't liked the city much at all. She'd moved to the west of Ireland, picked up with a Dutch painter, and married him. When Uncle Phil married Aunt Ruth, and found he was now related to an artist, he'd thought it all a bit strange. He wasn't quite sure what artists did, but he was certain that it wasn't actually work.

When Saskia's father began to get successful, Phil had seemed surprised. When he heard how much the paintings sold for, he'd seemed positively shocked. He couldn't make head or tail of the pictures that Saskia's father made. He was very nice about it, and really there was no harm in him, but Saskia felt sometimes that Phil regarded his artistic in-laws as creatures from another world.

The good thing about the visit was that Saskia would have lots of time with her cousin Simon. He was only a toddler, while Saskia was twelve, but he was the only cousin she had and she was very fond of him. She hadn't really seen much of Simon since they lived on opposite sides of the country; but apart from anything else she liked the idea of him. When she'd said as much once to Phil he'd seemed taken aback. 'But I suppose it's the sort of weird thing that she hears at home,' she'd heard him say later to Aunt Ruth. Saskia hadn't liked that; she didn't like people making allowances for her. She was what she was, and apologised to no-one for it. Her parents were happy that this was the case, and if Uncle Phil didn't like it he could ... well, he could do what he liked.

On Monday morning Saskia's mother and father drove her to the station in Galway and put her on the train with her suitcase and a pack of sandwiches. In the suitcase were three little pictures of her father's as a gift for Phil and Ruth.

'Uncle Phil won't like them, you know,' Saskia said to her father when she saw the paintings. 'He'll think they're just blots.'

'You might tell him what they're worth,' her mother said, smiling an evil smile. 'That will make him think again.'

'It will,' said Saskia. 'It will make him think the world is gone mad.'

She had a sarcastic tongue sometimes that she'd inherited from her mother. It ran in the family. It was another thing about her that sometimes unsettled her uncle. It reminded him, he'd once said, of Aunt Ruth in a bad mood. Even Saskia's father had complained one time that when the three women were together it was like having three witches ganging up on you. When he'd said that Phil had looked at him for once with real understanding.

'We'll see you in a few weeks,' her mother said now at the station.

'If I don't die of boredom first,' moaned Saskia. Her parents were flying to Amsterdam the next day. That was a city she did like, and she wasn't happy at missing the visit.

'*Hou op, mens,*' said her father warningly in Dutch. 'Keep a civil tongue in your head.'

Saskia grinned at him. 'Okay, I'll try not to shock poor old Phil,' she said.

'Try hard,' her mother said, warningly too. Then they both gave her kisses and hugs and got off the train. Saskia opened the window and stuck her head out. 'Don't drink too much, you two!' she called loudly down the platform after them. People looked around to see who the young girl was shouting at. Her father turned and grinned and shook his fist at her. Then they were gone, and the train started off for Dublin.

Saskia spent the journey worrying about her dreams. She'd been doing that a lot lately. She found her waking life full and fantastic, and couldn't imagine a life she'd prefer; but her dreams, in contrast, seemed always dull and drab. She couldn't remember when she'd first noticed this, but as time passed she'd come to worry about it more. By now she thought of it as her Problem, complete with a capital P. Her friends dreamed mad dreams of parties and flying – dreams that sounded really interesting. A typical Saskia dream, on the other hand, would be one where she peeled a sack of potatoes or something. Sometimes she even longed for a good old-fashioned nightmare – though mind you, peeling a sack of potatoes was nightmare enough in its own way.

It wasn't just her friends whose dreams were interesting either. Saskia had learned that with most people the situation was the opposite of her own: their dreams were much more interesting than their daily lives. This annoyed her. She felt she was missing out on something, and Saskia hated missing out on anything at all – barring potato-peeling and such. The visit to Ruth and Phil would no doubt be very dull; maybe then her dreams would seem more interesting, if only by comparison. She hoped they would, anyhow.

When the train reached the city the sandwiches were long gone and Saskia was just finishing the book she'd brought with her. It was a historical novel about a family trapped by fighting during the 1916 rebellion in Dublin. The book was interesting enough, but the boy who was the central figure got on Saskia's nerves. He was so sensible and at the same time so thick that Saskia felt someone should give him a good kick just to wake him up. She'd have done it herself if she'd been there. In the book the boy had two sisters, but they didn't do much apart from get sick, stand around or worry. They weren't, she'd decided early on, her kind of girls.

Uncle Phil was waiting in the station, still wearing his suit from work. He greeted her happily enough, and Saskia felt a bit ashamed of the way she'd been talking and thinking about him. Really, he was nice; it wasn't his fault if he was dull. And Saskia thought he looked exhausted.

'Have you been sick?' she asked him.

'Eh? No, no. But I'm very tired. We've been having some sleepless nights lately.'

'Is it Simon? Is he sick?'

Phil took her suitcase before answering. Then he seemed to consider her question. 'I don't think he is,' he said. 'But there's certainly something wrong with him.'

Saskia was concerned. 'Like what?' she asked.

Phil looked around at the bustling crowds. He shook his head wearily. 'Oh, I don't know,' he said. 'Let's just get out of here. I'll tell you all about it in the car.'

THE RACING CAR BED

The thing was, Phil said, that Simon had started having bad dreams. He'd wake up crying in the middle of the night. Phil or Ruth would go in to comfort him, but he always seemed terrified of going back to sleep. One of them would have to sit with him for an hour or more, reading stories and chatting while he had a warm drink. Then he'd drift off to sleep again, and sleep until morning.

There was nothing odd about this in itself: it happened now and then with every child. But these dreams had become a regular thing, and by now it was a real problem for Phil and Ruth. Both of them worked, and all the broken nights were leaving them tired and wretched by day. And of course they were worried about Simon too.

'There has to be a reason for it,' Phil had said to Ruth. 'Maybe it's something in the playschool.'

'I asked. They say he's fine up there.'

'Well it must be something else then.'

'The childcare book says it just happens sometimes.'

'But not every other night. Maybe we moved him to the big bed too soon.'

'Maybe.'

A few weeks ago – before any of the bad dreams – Simon had found out that he could climb out of his cot, which he'd promptly started to do. Phil and Ruth had been meaning to move him to a real bed anyway, but they hadn't got around to it yet. They were very busy people.

But one morning as they got up to go to work they'd met Simon playing on their steep stairs, and that had made up their minds for them.

'He'll break his neck climbing,' Ruth had said. 'Those stairgates we bought have been lying in the attic for six months. They go on tonight.'

'He can manage the stairs,' Phil said. 'It's climbing over the bars of the cot that I'm worried about. That's a high cot. He could break his neck if he fell there.'

'What about that bed you were going to build?'

Phil had had these big plans when Simon was younger. He was going to build his boy a proper bed himself, he'd say. Ruth, who was used to him, would laugh.

'You couldn't build a fire!' she'd say when he started on about it.

That would get Phil a bit annoyed, and he'd assure her that he was going to build Simon the best boy's bed in the world. It would be in the shape of a racing car, and Simon would love it.

'You'll never find the time, anyway,' she'd warn him. 'You can never find the time for anything.'

Now when they needed the big bed Phil still hadn't found the time. They couldn't even find the time to go and buy one. Then Ruth had seen a note on the noticeboard in the supermarket, offering a child's bed for sale.

'As new,' the sign said. 'Handmade child's bed in shape of racing car.'

'Brilliant!' she'd said to herself.

There was no telephone number on the note, so next evening after work they'd driven to the address it gave. They'd had a little trouble finding the place, but finally arrived at a lonely house just behind the park.

'Look at that,' Phil said. 'I never knew there was a house here.'

The house stood on its own in a big garden enclosed by hedges. It was more like a field than a garden. It bordered on the park itself. You could see the woods in the park rising above the back hedge. It was a lovely but lonely spot. There wasn't even a footpath on the road. The house itself was one of the old houses that had been there since before any of the housing estates were built. Phil had parked the car outside the high hedge and they'd looked through the little gate.

'What a nice old house,' Ruth said. 'I never noticed it before either.'

'This place must have been the middle of the country when that house was built,' Phil said dreamily. He'd been born down the country himself, and sometimes daydreamed of moving back there. Ruth had grown up in the city, and wasn't so sure.

The man who'd opened the door had been very old and very nice. He'd also been incredibly tall, and towered over both Ruth and Phil. He spoke in a tone hardly louder than a whisper. He wore dark, old-fashioned clothes, and a striped waistcoat over a collarless shirt. When he moved you could see braces peeping out of the gaps made in the stiff front of the waistcoat.

The old man had mild, watery blue eyes. He wore wire-rimmed spectacles. One of his cheeks was discoloured, covered by a large birthmark that was the shape and almost the colour of a strawberry.

The bed, the old man said, was supposed to be a present for his grandson. He'd built it himself, using skills that he'd learned as a boy.

'What went wrong?' Phil asked.

The old man looked terribly sad. 'An accident,' he said. 'Maybe I shouldn't say in front of the child.'

When they heard this Phil and Ruth had looked serious and troubled and understanding all at once. For a moment they'd been flustered. Then everybody nodded a lot and so Simon had nodded too, and nothing more had been said on the subject.

They loved the bed as soon as they saw it. It was just the kind Phil had wanted to make, only, to tell the truth, far better than anything he'd have been able to do. It was long and wide and low, and the sides and front were in the form of a blue racing car with a big number 3 and a go-faster stripe on the side. Simon had a thing about cars, and he loved it straight away too.

'For me!' he shouted. 'For me!'

The old man hadn't wanted much money for the bed. 'Just enough to cover the materials,' he said. 'I'd feel awkward making a profit out of it. I was just going to throw it out, to tell you the truth. But it would be nice to think someone was using it.'

The bed wouldn't fit in their car when the child-seat was

in, so Phil had dropped Ruth and Simon home, taken out the child-seat, and folded down the back seat of the car. Then he'd gone back and collected the bed.

'Money couldn't buy that kind of work nowadays,' Phil said at the time. 'There's real love went into that bed.'

'But it's awful to think of how it came to be for sale,' Ruth said. 'That poor old man. I'll never forget the way he looked when he mentioned the accident.'

'I liked the way he wouldn't talk about it in front of Simon. That was very thoughtful.'

Now, Phil told Saskia, they were having second thoughts about the big bed, though it was hard to see how the bed might be to blame for anything. Simon had loved the change from the very first. He seemed to feel that, now he was three, the big bed was a mark of his maturity. But certainly the dreams had only begun once he'd started sleeping in the new bed. There'd been three nights of peace after it arrived, and then the dreams had come. The two things mightn't be connected, but then again they might.

'I wish he could tell us what these dreams are about,' Phil had said to Ruth after the first few bad dreams.

'But he does tell us, or at least he tries to.'

'What? You mean that stuff about the green car? The Pooshipaw? That's not telling, is it? That's just rubbish.'

'Maybe your nightmares would sound like rubbish too if you just listed what happened in them. I know mine would.'

'Hmmm,' Phil had said. It was a thing he always said when he didn't know what to say.

'What's a Pooshipaw, anyway?' Ruth asked. 'It sounds like some bogeyman your mother might have mentioned to him.'

'Ma? She'd never scare him with talk like that. She's very careful. Maybe it's something he saw on the telly.'

'It doesn't sound like it. We'll probably never know.' She shook her head. 'Ooh,' she said, 'but I do wish he could really talk.'

A NIGHT ALARM

Aunt Ruth and Simon came to the door when they saw the car pull in. Simon was all over Saskia as soon as she got out. She loved the warm affection of his hugs. It was like holding some young, squirming animal in your arms.

'Simon!' Ruth said. 'Let Saskia get inside, at least.'

Uncle Phil got the suitcase from the boot of the car. Saskia noticed that Ruth looked as exhausted as he did, though it didn't dim the warmth of her welcome.

'How is your ma?' she asked Saskia.

'Grand. Busy. I hear you two are having trouble with Simon.'

'Oh ...' Ruth made a dismissive gesture. 'Yes. But I suppose it's part and parcel of being parents.'

Phil went straight upstairs with the case, while Simon hung out of Saskia. He knew she was his cousin, though he wasn't exactly clear on what a cousin was. He'd seen her house overlooking the sea, with a beach at the bottom of the garden, and he'd loved it.

'I hope I can get this fellow to bed tonight,' Ruth said. 'He's been so excited at your coming. He wants you to help with his bath.'

'And stories,' Simon said. 'Stories in bed.'

'For you, kid,' said Saskia, 'anything.'

Dinner was pleasant and Simon's bath a laugh. Saskia read him three bedtime stories, recited some Dutch nursery rhymes, and promised to play with him tomorrow. She gave him a big bedtime hug and closed his door, then went downstairs. Phil and Ruth were sitting in armchairs. They looked like they'd just run a marathon.

'You two are suffering more than he is,' she said.

'I know,' Ruth said. 'You wouldn't think to look at him that he was losing any sleep at all. But he is. And it's always the same dream, and we can't figure out what it is.'

'Did he have it last night?'

'No. Not for two nights now. Tonight might be the night. Then you'll see what we're talking about.'

'I've come at a bad time.'

'Lord, no. Maybe having you here will take his mind off whatever it is. Maybe he'll sleep through the night.'

But he didn't. His screams woke Saskia in the middle of the night. She lay in the dark in the little spare room and at first thought she was having a nightmare herself. Then she remembered where she was and realised what the screams must be. She jumped out of bed and met Phil and Ruth, looking dazed and frightened, in the hall.

When they went into Simon's room he was still screaming. Then he threw himself into Ruth's arms and the screams changed to sobs. Saskia was shocked. Simon was positively shaking with terror. She'd never seen anything like it. She looked at Phil. He was standing in his silly pyjamas with a look of utter helplessness on his face that made her pity him.

'But what does he dream about?' she asked.

'He was in the green car,' Phil said in a dull and mechanical way. 'He was driving it. The Pooshipaw was there. That's what he says every time we ask him – the same thing.'

'The Pooshipaw? What's that?'

'I have no idea. But just wait, you'll hear for yourself.'

By now Simon's sobs had subsided a little. He raised his red, tearful face to Saskia. 'I had a bad dream,' he said.

Saskia crouched down beside him and stroked his hair. It was clammy with sweat. 'What was it, chicken?' she asked him. 'What did you dream about?'

'I was in the green car,' he told her. 'And I was driving. And the Pooshipaw came.'

'But what's a Pooshipaw?'

'A Pooshipaw,' Simon said, 'is ... is a Pooshipaw.'

'That's about as much as you'll get from him,' Phil said. 'Believe me, we've tried.'

Saskia looked around. 'There's a funny kind of smell here,' she said.

'Nappies,' Phil suggested. 'He still wears one at night.'

'No. Something else.'

'Like what?'

Saskia sniffed. She shook her head. 'I don't know,' she said. 'It's gone now. Maybe it's something I just dreamed myself.'

'You go back to bed, love,' Ruth said to her. 'There's no point in all of us missing our sleep.'

'Why don't I take Simon with me? Maybe he'd like that.'

'Yes!' Simon said. 'Yes!'

Saskia saw Phil and Ruth exchange a glance. It was a strange mixture of temptation and concern. They wanted to sleep themselves, of course, they needed to. But they were concerned for her comfort too. Again Saskia felt a bit ashamed of things she'd thought about them.

'Look,' Phil said, 'we'll try it. If he keeps you awake then you can call us, and we'll put him back here and sit with him.'

So Saskia went back to her room with Simon trotting happily enough ahead of her. It was plain that her aunt and uncle were completely exhausted, and she was determined to stay up with Simon herself if she had to. After all, she didn't have to work the next day. But Simon lay quietly, holding her hand, seeming peaceful now.

Saskia fully intended staying awake until Simon slept, but she was very tired. In the end she fell asleep. Simon was still awake, but he knew that the Pooshipaw wouldn't come again now, not here, not when Saskia was with him. He lay awake for a while, secure beside the warmth of his cousin's body, thinking of the Pooshipaw, wishing that he could explain. He'd tried to explain the dreams to Mammy and Daddy, but they never understood. He talked very well for his age, but somehow he couldn't tell them about the worst things in the dreams. Even if he had been able to tell them, he somehow knew that they still wouldn't get it. There was no room in their world for the things in the dreams.

Simon liked everything to do with his Mammy and Daddy, but he wished they understood a little better what was happening to him. His favourite game had always been pretending to disappear. 'I'm going to go gone,' he'd shout. Then he'd cover his face with his hands and say, 'Now I'm gone,' and Mammy and Daddy would pretend they couldn't see him. But that was only a game: Simon didn't really want to go. He liked being with his Mammy and Daddy. He liked everything generally, in fact – except for the dreams.

Simon wished dearly that he could warn Mammy and Daddy about the dreams. You're my Mammy and Daddy, he wanted to say. You can do anything. And you'd better do something soon, because the Pooshipaw is going to make me drive away for ever in the green car. One day we'll be gone so far that there'll be nothing left behind. Nowadays Simon no longer played the game of going gone: it wasn't a game any more, but a fear.

After a long time that night Simon fell asleep. He had no more bad dreams – not that night.

THE POOSHIPAW

From the very first night, the Pooshipaw's visits had always been the same.

It had happened a couple of nights after Simon got the racing-car bed. He'd been sleeping peacefully when suddenly something woke him. At first he didn't know where he was, then he remembered that he was in the big new bed that Mammy and Daddy had bought. It was very comfortable. It was his bed now because he was a big boy.

The night lamp with its cartoon shade was lit with a dim light, and Simon lay on his back half-asleep, looking around his room at the familiar things. There were his bears and his box of toys, the mobiles hanging from the ceiling and the paper frieze of tumbling clowns that ran all around the walls. The only thing in the room that had changed was the bed.

Then Simon heard a low beeping. He wondered what it was. Soon he realised that it was coming from the bed itself. He wanted to sit up, but he couldn't. He was still half-asleep.

'What's that?' he said.

Then the beeping stopped. Simon felt a weight on the bottom of the bed. He heard someone yawning noisily.

'Ah, musha,' said a voice that creaked. 'No rest for the wicked.'

When Simon looked down he saw a peculiar creature sitting at the bottom of his bed. It was very short and very fat, and didn't really look like anything he'd ever seen before.

The creature was shaped a bit like a dustbin, and it had a huge head. Its head and body were covered in fur of a funny colour like a cross between orange and green. It wore a big overcoat from which the sleeves had been torn; you could still see the threads hanging from where they'd been ripped. The overcoat was shiny with grease, and it smelled very dirty. The creature looked around the room and then turned to Simon, scratching itself. As it turned Simon noticed that its arms were bare of fur, though they too were green. The arms were strongly muscled, and there was something odd about them that Simon couldn't quite make out. Then he saw that the oddity wasn't so much in the arms as in the hands that were at the ends of them: the creature had two left hands.

'Howya, Sausage,' the creature said. 'What's your name?'

'Simon,' Simon said.

The creatured giggled. 'So,' he said. 'Simon!' He pointed a clawed finger at Simon. 'Before the cock crows twice,' he said, 'you will deny me thrice. Or is it the other way round?' He giggled again. 'Divil the bit of good it will do you anyhow,' he said.

'What do you want?' Simon asked.

'Dear Sausage Simon,' said the creature. 'I'm going to give you the keys to my kingdom. Such as it is.' Then he giggled again. It wasn't a nice giggle.

'Who are you?' Simon said.

The creature was wearing a very large and very battered

hat on top of his very large and very furry head. He scratched under the hat before answering.

'Questions, questions, questions,' he said. 'But I don't mind. I, Simon, am the Pooshipaw.'

'What's a Pooshipaw?'

The Pooshipaw considered. 'Do you know,' he said, 'I don't think there's words for it. Pooshipaw is as Pooshipaw does, I always say. I'm just ... the Pooshipaw.'

'Why are your two hands the same?' Simon asked.

The Pooshipaw looked surprised. He held up his powerful arms and looked at his hands. They were very big hands, with claws at the ends of the green fingers.

'I'm an unnatural creature,' the Pooshipaw said. He didn't sound worried by the fact. 'A sinister creature, you might say. Do you know any Latin, Simon?'

'What's a Latin?' Simon asked.

The Pooshipaw giggled. 'I'm sorry, Sausage,' he said. 'I asked a foolish question. Latin is a language, Simon, and the Latin word for "left" is *sinister*. So you see, I suppose my maker left this mark to remind me that that's what I am – sinister.'

'And what's sinister?'

The Pooshipaw made a face. He sighed. 'Sometimes I forgets,' he said, 'just how ignorant youse are.'

He flexed his two left hands in front of Simon's face, waggling the clawed green fingers. 'Just look, Sausage,' he said. 'Now, don't you think that looks scary?'

Simon looked. The hands did look sort of scary, he supposed, but mostly they just looked strange. It must be awkward having two left hands, or two right ones for that matter. Still, the Pooshipaw seemed anxious that he should be frightened, and Simon was an obliging child.

'I suppose so,' he said, trying to sound afraid. 'Is that what sinister is – scary?'

The Pooshipaw heard the effort in his voice, and got annoyed. 'Be the living jinnet, sonny boy,' he said, 'be the time I'm finished with you, you'll know exactly what sinister is.'

There was a dark threat in his voice, and suddenly Simon didn't want to know any more about the meaning of the word.

'This is my room,' he said.

'But of course,' said the Pooshipaw softly. 'Of course it is, Sausage. Who else's would it be?'

The Pooshipaw got off the bed and stood looking around the room with a sneer on his face. 'Very pretty,' he said. 'Very nice. But I suppose it will do.'

He came over and squatted on the floor by the bed. He grunted with the effort. 'Stiff,' he said. 'Stiff and sore.'

Simon still couldn't seem to move. The Pooshipaw leaned over him and looked at his face. He ruffled the little boy's fair hair. 'Such a pretty child,' he said. 'Like your new bed, do you, Sausage?'

'Yes,' Simon said. 'It's a racing car.'

The Pooshipaw looked at the side of the bed. 'Begob,' he said, 'so it is! We moves with the times, I suppose. We keeps abreast of developments.'

He took a bone out of his pocket. Simon saw that the bone was covered with dirt and earth. Things were crawling on it, nasty-looking things.

'I prefer more leisurely times meself,' the Pooshipaw said. 'All this modern rushing around would make me dizzy. Rush, rush, rush! And for what? The same ould place that youse all end up.'

He looked critically at the bone, then sucked it. 'Ah!' he said. 'That's good, that is. Juicy.'

He looked in Simon's eyes. His own eyes, large and yellow, seemed to light up with a cloudy light. 'The Pooshipaw likes to take its time,' he said. 'Humans are after forgetting how to do that. But then, of course, they have so little of it anyway.'

He raised the bone and waved it in the air as though writing there. Simon saw smoky marks hanging in the air where the bone passed. He'd never seen anything like that before.

'What is the world,' said the Pooshipaw, 'if, full of care, we have no time to stop and stare.'

The writing hovered for a moment and then vanished.

'Are you a dog?' Simon asked. 'Or maybe a cat?'

It seemed a reasonable enough question. The Pooshipaw didn't exactly look like either a dog or a cat, but he looked more like a dog or a cat than like anything else Simon had ever seen.

But the Pooshipaw didn't seem to like the question at all. He sniffed.

'Or a bear,' Simon said. 'Are you a bear?' Because there was a certain resemblance there, too.

'Hmmph,' said the Pooshipaw. 'I suppose at least it's better nor a cat.'

He put the whole bone in his mouth and crunched it. Simon was astonished. It was a very big bone. That was the first time, too, that he saw the Pooshipaw's great yellow teeth.

'What I am,' the Pooshipaw said, 'is a class of a monster.'

The idea didn't frighten Simon as such. He'd seen lots of nice monsters on television. But he knew immediately that the Pooshipaw wasn't nice.

'I don't like you,' he said.

The Pooshipaw crunched and swallowed. 'That,' he said, 'is neither here nor there. I can't say I'm mad about you either – a cat, indeed! Still, I'm sure we can work together. Our relationship is strictly a business one. We don't have to like one another.'

'I'm going to go gone,' Simon said, and covered his face with his hands.

The Pooshipaw grinned down at him with his yellow fangs.

'You never spoke a truer word, Sausage,' he crooned. 'That's exactly what you're going to do. But enough chit-chat. Let's go for a drive.'

And suddenly they weren't in the bedroom any more. They weren't in the house at all. They were in a car, and now Simon was really frightened. It was partly because of the sudden change, but it was mostly because he was driving the car. Desperately he turned the steering wheel this way and that, as he'd seen Mammy and Daddy do in their own car. He wasn't sure what turning the wheel did, but it seemed to work when he did it: the car kept going.

The car drove under a big sign that was stretched across the road. The sign was painted brightly. Written on it in large letters were the words START HERE – GOODBYE! Simon knew they were words because they looked like the words in the storybooks Mammy and Daddy read for him, but he didn't know what the words said because he couldn't read yet.

The words on the sign were the least of Simon's worries. He was terrified of the driving, and he had no idea how to stop a car. He was driving down a narrow road with a high hedge on each side. The hedges were so high that their tops almost met overhead, so that sometimes he seemed to be driving through a kind of tunnel. He was afraid to take his eyes off the road, but he sensed someone sitting in the passenger seat beside him.

'What do you say, Sausage?' asked the voice of the Pooshipaw.

'I want to stop,' Simon said. 'I want my Mammy and Daddy.'

'Pshaw!' said the Pooshipaw. 'There's no Mammies and Daddies here, kid. Not as such, anyhow. Here you have to stand on your own two feet. You can do that, can't you?'

'I'm a big boy!' Simon said.

'Sure you are, Sausage,' said the Pooshipaw. 'Sure you are.'

Driving frightened Simon because he didn't know what he was doing. On the floor of Mammy and Daddy's car, under the steering wheel, there were pedals that the driver pushed with his feet. Simon's feet didn't reach to the floor of this car, and he couldn't look down for pedals because he was so afraid of taking his eyes off the road.

What he really wanted to do was to take his hands off the steering wheel, because that might stop the car. But his hands seemed stuck to the wheel, so he just kept turning it.

Everything Simon could see of the car, inside and out, was coloured a dark green. The driver's seat was very high, and might have been built up specially for someone his age.

'Where are we going?' he asked the Pooshipaw.

'Over the hills and far away,' the Pooshipaw said.

'Hills?' Simon asked. He could see no hills, but then, because of the hedges, he could see very little apart from the road itself.

'Janey!' said the Pooshipaw. 'It's only a line from a song, kid. Young people nowadays knows nothing. You never mind where we're going. We're going where I'm taking you. You just keep your eyes on the road.'

The Pooshipaw started to sing to himself. He would sing a snatch of a song and then another, but never finish any of them. He had a terrible voice.

'Up on a mountain,' sang the Pooshipaw, 'that's the place to be, listenin' to a jackass singin' in a tree.'

With each passing moment Simon grew more frightened. He was old enough to know that there was something very wrong going on here. In the back seat the Pooshipaw started to sing 'Boolavogue' in a voice so cracked that even the Pooshipaw seemed to feel he had to excuse it.

'The ould pipes is rusty,' he said. 'They're out of practice.'

They passed a road sign with a black border. ACCIDENT BLACK SPOT, the sign said, though of course Simon couldn't read it. Suddenly they turned a tight bend in the road with a broad grassy patch beyond it. Another car was lying over-turned on the grassy patch. It looked very like Daddy's and Mammy's car. There was smoke coming out of it.

Two people were lying on the grass beside the smoking car. One of the people was a man, the other one was a woman. The man was Daddy. The woman was Mammy. They were lying very awkwardly, and they were very, very still.

Simon wanted to stop the green car, but he didn't know how. It turned around another bend and left the crashed car behind.

'Mmmm,' said the Pooshipaw dreamily. 'That reminds me. I'm hungry.'

Simon screamed and screamed and screamed. Then he was back in his bed and the Pooshipaw was gone. Mammy came running into his room in her nightdress. That was the first night, the easiest one.

MONSTER AT WORK

From then on the Pooshipaw had come every few nights or
so, and each time he came Simon had the bad dream. Every
dream involved driving in the green car, and with each drive
the distance they drove grew greater. The landscape never
changed: they were always driving down an endless narrow
road lined with high green hedges. But the farther down that
road they travelled, the more sick and frightening were the
scenes at the roadside; and with every dream Simon grew
more afraid.

Somehow Simon knew that the journey in the green car
had an end, and that with each dream that end grew closer.
What was waiting at the end he didn't know, but from the
first he was sure that it was nothing nice. He doubted that
anything involving the Pooshipaw could be nice.

Daddy and Mammy had quizzed Simon endlessly about
the bad dreams, trying to find out what caused them. Simon
had told them what he could, but they could make no sense
of it. This was hardly surprising – Simon could make no sense
of it either.

He did try to tell Mammy and Daddy that there was more
to it than just dreams, that the Pooshipaw actually brought
the dreams and in some way made him dream them. But he'd
found that he couldn't explain that the Pooshipaw came
before the dreams and not just in them. It was a hard idea for
him to express, but there was more than just that. Whenever

he tried to say something about it a strange thing happened: the words got as far as his mouth, but they wouldn't come out. Simon suspected that the Pooshipaw was responsible for this, though he didn't know how.

As time passed the Pooshipaw started to chat for longer before beginning the bad dreams, though 'chat' wasn't really the right word: it was mostly a case of the Pooshipaw talking to himself. He seemed to love the sound of his own voice. Then again, Simon gathered that he didn't often have someone to talk to. The life of a Pooshipaw seemed to be a lonely one, really, and in spite of himself Simon started to pity the creature a little bit.

Simon knew that he shouldn't feel sympathy for the Pooshipaw, that he should be afraid of him. He didn't know what the creature was, nor how it had come to him, but from early on the Pooshipaw made no secret of what he wanted. What he wanted was to take Simon away from Mammy and Daddy, to take him away to a faraway, dark place where there was no-one that Simon knew. The Pooshipaw seemed to enjoy the prospect of doing this.

So Simon tried hard to be afraid of the Pooshipaw, but somehow he wasn't able. The Pooshipaw had tried to explain this to him.

'It's called numbing your faculties,' he said.

'What's that?' Simon asked.

'I haven't a bull's notion how it works,' the Pooshipaw admitted. 'I was never very technical. But it means you're not able to be properly afraid. You're sort of hypnotised. But I suppose you don't know what that means either. I'm no good at explaining. It's not part of my job.'

Instead of the Pooshipaw it was the dreams that Simon was afraid of, even though he knew that the Pooshipaw brought them. By now he knew too that they weren't really dreams, that they were something more than that; but there was nothing else he could call them.

'Dreams is as good a name as any,' the Pooshipaw said. 'Any road, it makes no differ in the end. It'll be a dream of you I take away, you could say, and a dream of you will be all your precious Mammy and Daddy have left.'

The Pooshipaw didn't like Mammies and Daddies. He didn't seem to like any grown-ups, really. And although he always talked nicely enough to Simon, and called him pet names, still it seemed to Simon that the Pooshipaw didn't like children either. The Pooshipaw didn't seem to like anyone.

'It's not my job to like people,' he'd said when Simon asked. 'And I *am* my job, pal. That's something you should remember about me: I lives for my work. Anyway,' he said, 'I don't see much in people to like. You're young, you don't know them very well. Really, I'm doing you a favour taking you away from all this.'

By now the Pooshipaw sometimes came when Simon wasn't in bed. It didn't happen often, but you never knew where he might turn up. He'd even come several times when either Mammy or Daddy was there, and it was obvious that they couldn't see or hear him. The one thing Simon noticed was that he never came by day. He didn't seem to like daytime much.

'It shows up all them nice places and smiley people,' he told Simon. 'Dark is better. Dark is for secrets, Sausage.'

Oddly enough the Pooshipaw seemed to have no fear of light itself. One night Simon even met him in the supermarket, where the lights were very bright. Simon was sitting in the big shopping trolley while Mammy drove him around. She'd parked him near the petfood while she went to weigh the vegetables.

'Hey, Sausage!' someone said, and when Simon looked around, there was the Pooshipaw. He was holding his overcoat open and stuffing cans of dogfood into the inside pocket. It was funny in a way to see how deftly he did it, considering that he had two left hands. He held the left side of his overcoat open with what should have been his right hand, but wasn't; with the other hand he grabbed the cans of dogfood and crammed them in.

'Nothing like a bit of shopping,' the Pooshipaw said. 'It gets a body out and about. You learn to know your local community, like.'

Simon was watching the cans of dogfood. The Pooshipaw was stuffing more and more in, but the pocket didn't even bulge. It seemed bottomless.

The Pooshipaw saw where Simon was looking. 'That's a fine big pocket,' he said. 'You don't find workmanship like that nowadays. That's where I puts little boys and girls, you know – when I've done with them. I folds them up like paper bags and puts them right there next to my heart, where it's nice and dark and cosy.'

'Have you a dog?' Simon asked.

'Eh?' said the Pooshipaw. Then he cackled. 'No, no,' he said. 'But I'm partial betimes to a can of the beef and liver. One of the few half-dacent foods in your rotten shops, and yiz gives it to animals!'

He thought for a moment. '"Have you a dog" indeed!' he said. 'I suppose it's a step up from asking me whether I'm a cat.'

Later that night, when he turned up in the bedroom, he had an open can of beef-and-liver dogfood in his hand or paw – Simon could never decide which it was.

'Well,' the Pooshipaw said. The fur around his mouth glistened with crushed dogfood. 'Here we are again.'

He tipped back his great head and opened his mouth wide. He held the can upside down over his mouth and shook it. The dogfood, shiny with jelly, began to fall out slowly in the form of a neat tube. It made an odd sucking sound as it came. After a while it dropped into the Pooshipaw's mouth. He closed his mouth and chewed noisily. Then he swallowed with a loud gulp and smacked his great, rubbery lips.

'Aaah!' he said. He smiled at Simon with his big teeth. 'So how's my boy?' he said.

'I want a well-earned rest,' Simon said. It was a phrase that he'd heard Daddy use.

The Pooshipaw's smile got wider. 'You'll have rest enough soon,' he said. 'Plenty and plenty of rest. Right now it's time to work.'

And with no warning they were in the green car, and already Simon was looking for the strength to scream.

MEDICAL ADVICE

The day after Saskia came, Simon stayed home from playschool. While Phil and Ruth were at work, Saskia took him into the city on a bus. They visited an art gallery and fed the ducks in the park, and Simon was delighted with the day. He showed no signs of distress from the night before. A couple of times Saskia tried to question him gently about his dreams, but he just told her the same things she'd already heard.

When Phil and Ruth got home that evening they looked more tired than ever. Saskia, whose mother and father had been teaching her to cook things for as long as she could remember, had made dinner for them. It was an Indonesian meal she'd made from things she'd found in the cupboard. Aunt Ruth, who did all the cooking in the house, looked at her especially gratefully.

Although they both made admiring noises about dinner, Phil and Ruth seemed too exhausted to actually enjoy it. They went so far as to apologise to Saskia for their lack of appreciation.

'We just can't keep this up,' Phil said. 'I nearly fell asleep at my desk today.'

'Maybe we should take him to a doctor,' Ruth said.

Phil thought about that. 'Yes,' he said suddenly. 'What's more, I'll do it this very night. Doctor Murray has an evening surgery.'

'Good Lord,' said Ruth, with some mockery showing even through her tiredness. 'I love it when you're all decisive. It's not like you.'

'I'm not being decisive,' Phil admitted. 'I'm being desperate.'

After dinner he put Simon in the car. Simon didn't mind going, but only if Saskia went too. Saskia had no objections.

Doctor Murray examined Simon and found nothing wrong.

'Can nothing be done?' Phil asked. 'We're going daft with the sleepless nights.'

The doctor held his hands up in a gesture of helplessness. 'I can find nothing organic,' he said. 'I'll send him for tests if it makes you feel better, but I think the results will confirm my diagnosis. I could give you some sleeping pills for yourselves, but that wouldn't solve the problem – you'd still have a crying child.'

'But what can it be?' Phil asked. He really did sound

desperate. Again the doctor made the helpless gesture. What can I say?' he asked. 'It's a phase he's going through. It happens.'

'A phase?' Phil sounded almost angry.

Doctor Murray shrugged. 'I didn't say it was a nice phase,' he said.

Saskia, who hadn't been introduced to the doctor, looked from one of them to the other. The doctor had a neat beard, and looked very, very clean. Phil's eyes looked a bit wild. Actually, she thought, it suited him in a way: it made him look more human.

'What about a child psychologist?' Phil asked.

The doctor made a face. 'Yes,' he said, 'there are child psychologists, but' – he pointed at Simon – 'this child is three years old. From what you tell me, and what I know of your family, he lives in perfectly normal surroundings. There's no reason to think he's mentally disturbed in any way.'

Phil nodded and sighed. 'It's myself and his mother who are getting disturbed,' he said. Then he looked at Simon and smiled. He ruffled the child's hair. 'Don't get me wrong, doctor,' he said. 'We know we're very lucky with the little fella. But the lack of sleep is a killer.'

'Why don't you all take a holiday or something?' the doctor suggested. 'I know you both work. Maybe it's an insecure phase that he's going through, and he just needs to see more of you.'

Phil thought about that. 'Do you know,' he said, 'that might be a good idea. I think Ruth has some holidays due. I know I have.'

'That sounded like the sort of advice a child psychologist might give,' Saskia said to the doctor.

The doctor smiled.

'This is Saskia,' Phil said, 'Simon's cousin. Her father's a painter,' he added, as though excusing her for something.

'That's adult psychology, Saskia,' the doctor said. 'I've been a doctor for twenty-five years. You pick up a bit as you go along.'

Phil smiled too. He smiled at the doctor and he smiled at Saskia. Then he smiled down at Simon. But Simon was looking over to the corner of the room, where the Pooshipaw was sitting, licking something that looked like blood off his eight left fingers and two left thumbs. He looked bored.

The Pooshipaw felt Simon's glance and looked back at him. He grinned. He could be very winning in his ways when he wanted to be, but Simon hated his grin. His mouth stretched from one ear to the other, and when he smiled Simon always thought the top of his head was going to fall off. Then again his teeth were like knives, and there always seemed to be blood on them.

'What a lot of ould guff they do talk,' said the Pooshipaw. 'Don't they?'

Neither Saskia nor Daddy heard it speak, nor did the doctor. They couldn't see it either. Grown-ups couldn't ever see the Pooshipaw. Simon had asked the monster about this, and the Pooshipaw had told him that grown-ups couldn't see it because they didn't believe it was there.

'They're funny like that,' the Pooshipaw said. 'They only see what they believe.'

Now the Pooshipaw looked from Daddy to the doctor and sighed.

'What fools these mortals be,' he said to no-one in particular. Then he blew his nose in his fingers with a jeering sound.

'We'll be off, so,' Phil said to Doctor Murray.

'What about those tests?' the doctor asked. 'Do you want

me to arrange them for you?'

Phil thought about it. 'No,' he said. 'I'm sure you're right. We're just getting so desperate, you know? But I think the idea of a holiday is good. Nothing exotic, just a week in the country at my mother's. A bit of relaxation. What do you say, Saskia? Would you fancy a week in the country?'

'Is the Pope a Catholic?' Saskia asked, but that just seemed to confuse Phil so she changed it to 'Yes!'

The doctor nodded several times. 'Good,' he said. 'Excellent. You can leave my fee with the receptionist,' he said to Phil.

'To be sure,' Phil replied.

Meanwhile the Pooshipaw was standing on a chair looking with a professional eye through the contents of a medicine cabinet on the wall. He turned to Simon as they left and tipped his hat to him.

'See yeh later, kiddo,' he said. 'We'll go for a drive.'

Simon only stopped crying when they got to the car. Phil shook his head. 'Lord,' he said to Saskia, 'I never saw him blow up like that before. Sometimes lately I wonder what gets into him.'

'Beeps,' Simon said. 'Beeps get into me.'

But Phil just laughed. He couldn't help it. He thought it was one of those childish statements that adults find so funny.

'So the beeps get into you, do they?' he said. 'I must remember to tell that one to your Ma.'

The suggestion of a holiday seemed to have cheered him up a lot. Saskia wondered why he hadn't thought of it himself.

'We'll go,' he said, 'to see my mother.'

'Will she mind me coming along?'

'Lord, no. She'd be delighted. She's actually very curious about you.'

Saskia liked the idea of getting out of the city so soon. 'I'm all for it,' she said. 'What about you, Simon? Would you like to get away?'

'Yes,' Simon said, and he sounded positively eager. 'I would, yes.'

MOVING THE GOALPOSTS

Simon's Nanny lived in a snug bungalow in the southeast. The bungalow stood on its own by the road just outside a village. There was a little gravelled yard in front and a big back garden with apple trees. All around were green fields. The house itself was very old, and at various times people had added bits and pieces on to it until it was a maze of odd-shaped rooms. Phil's family had lived there for a very long time.

Simon loved exploring Nanny's house. All of the rooms had a friendly air off them. The house was full of odd bits and pieces, and everything seemed to welcome his attention. Sometimes when they were there Ruth or Phil would give out to him for touching things, but Nanny always hushed them.

'Go away out of that,' she'd say. 'Let the child play. It's how they learns.'

'But Ma,' Phil might say, 'that's a piece of Waterford crystal! That's valuable!'

'Yerra,' Nanny would say, 'what's more valuable nor a child's curiosity?'

Then Phil and Ruth would stop bothering Simon, though when Nanny wasn't around they'd fret about her easy-going ways.

'The child has to learn respect for other people's property,' Ruth would say. 'We won't be able to take him anywhere.'

'I know,' Phil would say. 'I know. But you won't persuade Ma of that.'

'Oh well,' Ruth would say doubtfully. 'I suppose it's a grandparent's privilege to spoil a child a bit.'

There were several things about Simon's Nanny that Ruth and Phil disapproved of. They both loved her dearly, but she was old-fashioned, they said, and superstitious. They thought that she gave Simon bad habits. She'd never read a childcare book in her life.

Simon, on the other hand, could see nothing wrong with his Nanny at all. He was almost as fond of her as he was of Mammy and Daddy.

Nanny was very old. She was a small, stout woman who glowed with a comforting air of love, especially for Simon. Her eyes lit up when she looked at him. Simon always felt completely safe with her.

As the time for the visit came closer Simon got very excited. He knew exactly where he was going. He'd have been delighted anyway, but the prospect of going there with Saskia too made it all twice as nice. And he'd discovered that the Pooshipaw couldn't follow, which would make it all perfect.

The bad dreams didn't stop, but still they didn't seem to be affecting Simon's daytime life. Ruth and Phil were going through their days half-asleep, but at the prospect of leaving the city even they seemed to relax.

'Do you think he'll have the dreams down there?' Ruth asked at breakfast the day before they left.

'Who knows?' Phil said. 'But with Saskia and Ma we'll have two babysitters every evening. We can go to the pub in the village.'

'And you should go,' said Saskia. 'You're both in bad need of a rest.'

'And daytrips to the sea!' Ruth sighed. She turned to Simon in his high chair. 'You'll like that, Simon,' she said. 'The sea!'

'The sea,' Simon said. It was a lovely idea, though of course Nanny didn't have the sea at the bottom of her garden, like Saskia did.

The Pooshipaw didn't like the idea of Simon going away at all. This would be the first time Simon had gone to Nanny's since the dreams started. The Pooshipaw said that Mammy and Daddy were cheating. Moving the goalposts, he called it.

'It's undoing my work,' he complained for the twentieth time to Simon that night. 'I don't mind the wasted time myself – far from it. But I have a tight schedule, you know.'

He coughed up some phlegm into his hand, examined it, then licked it up.

'Waste not, want not,' he said. He made a face at Simon. 'Your parents have no consideration,' he said.

'You're a busy man,' Simon said to the Pooshipaw. It was a phrase that he'd heard Mammy use to Daddy. Saying it now to the Pooshipaw, he used the joking tone of voice that Mammy used when she said it.

The Pooshipaw didn't seem to like him saying it at all. 'That's insulting,' he said. 'I'm not a man, I'm a Pooshipaw. But aye, as it happens, I'm busy. I have my timetable to think of.'

The Pooshipaw was sitting at the bottom of the racing-car bed, chewing one of the bones that he kept in his pockets for when he got hungry in the night. Simon didn't know where the Pooshipaw got the bones, but they were always raw and dirty as though they'd come out of a butcher's rubbish bin.

'That's dirty,' Simon said.

The Pooshipaw looked at the gnawed bone. His great teeth had crunched it like hard toffee. 'Ain't it, though?' he said, smiling with the big teeth.

Mammy and Daddy had told Simon that they'd all be getting up very early next morning. The bags were packed and standing in the hall. Now Simon asked the Pooshipaw whether he could please skip the dreams tonight, because Mammy and Daddy could really use a good night's sleep.

When he asked the question the Pooshipaw seemed to cheer up. He got his sly smile on and his sulphur-coloured eyes turned up in his head as they always did when he was thinking.

'Do you know,' he said to Simon, 'I'm getting slow. I never thought of that. This would be an awful night for them to spend up, wouldn't it?'

And Simon knew then that he'd said the wrong thing, that the Pooshipaw would make tonight's dreams especially scary.

'You're not nice,' Simon said.

The Pooshipaw had finished the bone. He examined his fingers for grease and sucked them noisily before answering. Then he cleared his throat with a sick sound, took off his hat and spat in it before putting it back on.

'No, Sausage,' he said, sounding very pleased with himself. 'I'm not nice at all.'

NANNY'S

'Yiz look shattered,' was the first thing Simon's Nanny said when they arrived at her house.

'We were up half the night with Simon,' Phil said. 'Bad dreams. Then he woke again after. If Saskia hadn't taken him into bed with her, I think we might have been up all night. We were nearly not coming, we were that whacked.'

They were in her front yard. Simon was asleep in his child-seat in the back of the car. Nanny peered in at him through the car window.

'He looks peaceful enough now,' she said.

'He conked out the minute we left the city,' Ruth said. 'So did I. Then halfway down I took over the driving and let his dad get some sleep. But we're all in bits.'

'Such a night for it to happen,' Phil said. 'And twice in the one night, too. I hope it's not getting worse. If it starts happening every night then we're in real trouble.'

'Oh?' Nanny said. 'And how long has this been going on?'

'A month or so. Since we got the new bed for him.'

'You never told me anything about it,' Nanny said. She sounded faintly accusing.

'Not a lot you could do, Ma, was there?' Phil said. 'We brought him to a doctor – thought he might be sick or something. But no joy.'

Nanny looked in at Simon again. 'He's peaceful enough now anyhow,' she said. 'Maybe it was changing the bed. They likes things to be regular. Childer are very conservative.'

Ruth smiled at the notion of Simon's Nanny calling someone else conservative. Ruth tended to think that old people down the country lived in another century.

Distracted as they were by Simon's problems no-one had introduced Saskia yet. Saskia didn't mind. It gave her a few minutes to take stock of Phil's mother. She liked what she saw – a small, stocky woman with a friendly, wrinkled face. 'A lived-in face', her father called faces like that. Then the lived-in face turned to her and smiled a smile that warmed her.

'And this must be young Saskia,' the face said. 'And it's very welcome you are, dear, to my house.'

Saskia shook hands and said hello. She liked the woman immediately. You could see she was lively. Saskia had half-expected Phil's mother to be a dry old stick of a thing – like her son, Saskia was tempted to think. But she could see straight away that this woman was nothing like that.

They decided to let Simon sleep in the car for a little while. He'd be all the better for it, Ruth said. Nanny said she had to go in to the village for a few messages.

'Wait till Simon wakes up,' Phil said, 'and I'll drive you in.'

'Yerra, not at all. It's only down the road. I meant to go in this morning, only Birdie Murray called.'

'Birdie Murray?' Phil said. 'Is she still alive?'

'Alive and thriving,' Nanny said. 'And she ninety-five years of age. She still rides the same bike.'

'You're joking,' Phil said.

'Indeed and I'm not. The same ould high nellie.'

Ruth made a face as she carried in a bag. When they were in Nanny's house Phil often spent time discussing people she'd never heard of with his mother. It was like a kind of ritual.

Nanny went to the village on foot in spite of Phil's repeated offer to drive her.

'I'll be a little while,' she said. 'Youse make yourselves some tea. There's a cake in the biscuit tin in the kitchen, and ham for sandwiches in the fridge.'

They took all the luggage in quietly and then had tea and cake at the kitchen table. Ruth made sandwiches with the great, thick slices of country ham. From the kitchen window they could see Simon in the car.

'Who's Birdie Murray?' Ruth asked. She liked to show an interest.

Phil laughed and shook his head. 'When I was young,' he said, 'we all thought she was a witch.'

Ruth sniggered.

'Oh go ahead,' Phil said. 'Laugh. But you should see her. This straight old widow in black, living alone in a weird old cottage up a lane. A very peculiar woman. She used to go around on this amazing old bike – it looked about six feet tall. Everyone was afraid of her. I mean, they were friendly to her and all, but they used to say ...' He shook his head again, smiling.

'What?' Ruth asked.

'Well, they used to say that she was friendly with the fairies.'

Ruth snorted. 'Really!' she said. 'In the nineteen sixties!'

'The seventies, please,' said Phil, who was getting to an age where he was sensitive about how old he was.

Saskia had been looking out at Simon. 'Your son and heir is stirring,' she said. 'Shall I get him?'

She ran out without waiting for an answer. Ruth smiled after her. 'She loves that child,' she said.

'Who wouldn't?' asked Phil. 'But I must say she's very good with him. She's been a real help this last week.'

'Even if she's been brought up wild?' Ruth smirked, quoting something he'd said to her once.

Phil grunted.

Simon woke up with a smile on his face. He knew exactly where he was. He'd smelled the faint trace of Nanny's house in his sleep, and had dreamed a sweet dream in which the Pooshipaw had turned into his friend. When Saskia opened the car door he smiled and trilled at her: 'We're hee-re!'

'Yes we are, kiddo,' Saskia said. 'We surely are.'

She undid the straps of his car-seat and took a deep breath of the sweet country air. She was enjoying herself.

When they went inside Simon ran from room to room looking for his Nanny.

'She's in the shop,' Ruth said.

'Buying a prezzie,' said Simon.

'Oh you think so, do you?'

'An icepop,' Simon said.

Ruth and Phil laughed.

'I wouldn't mind,' Ruth said, 'but she probably is. We mustn't let her spoil him too much this time.'

'Oh,' Phil said, 'what the hell. We're on our holidays.'

Simon was charging around the place doing amateur gymnastics. Ruth sighed as she watched.

'Look at him,' she said. 'Awake half the night, and full of beans now.'

'I just hope he doesn't wake tonight,' Phil said. 'I'd give my right arm for a good night's sleep.'

Ruth laughed. 'You'll snore through the night,' she said. 'And there I'll be, lying awake in dread of fairies and ninety-five year old witches.'

'She wasn't that kind of witch,' Phil said. 'Birdie was a wise woman, a good witch.'

Ruth looked at him. 'My God!' she said. 'Sometimes I wonder what I married into.'

Simon was pulling at Saskia's hand. 'We have to say hello to Tiger Mike,' he said. Saskia looked questioningly at his parents.

Phil grinned. 'He always has to do that,' he said. 'Go on, he'll show you around. It's the room you'll be sleeping in, anyhow.'

When they'd gone he was still grinning. 'You mock on,' he said to Ruth. 'But if that little devil has us up all night again tonight I'll be up to Birdie Murray in the morning to see if she knows a cure for Pooshipaws.'

Ruth laughed. 'True enough,' she said. 'And I'll be right behind you.'

TIGER MIKE

Simon's Nanny was one of those people who keep things long after they have no use for them. A hoarder, Ruth and Phil called her. As well as the things lying around the house there were all sorts of bits and pieces stashed away in drawers and cupboards, wrapped in plastic bags. You never knew, she thought, when you might need something.

When she'd said that to Phil he'd made a face. 'Never,' he said, 'is exactly when you will need half this stuff.'

Ruth and Phil agreed that Nanny's hoarding was one of her bad habits, though like all her other bad habits it was a harmless one. Simon didn't think hoarding was a bad habit at all. The oddities scattered around the house were one of the most interesting things about it. You never knew what Nanny was going to produce from the depths of a cupboard, wrapped in a bag stamped with the name of some shop that had closed twenty years ago.

Among the things Nanny had kept were old toys belonging to Phil and his sister Mary.

'Though they're mostly Mary's,' she said when they were mentioned. 'Philip was never a one for keeping things in one piece for long. He'd only to look at a toy to break it.'

Still there were lots of toys kept in the back bedroom that once had been Phil's. Simon was too young to play with some of them, but there was a whole box of soft toys that he loved to talk to. The toys seemed to like him too.

There were teddies and clowns and animals in the box, and several of Mary's old dolls. One stuffed animal in particular, though, was Simon's favourite. It was a big tiger, nearly half a metre long, and it had great friendly lemon-coloured eyes.

'Philip's uncle Mike, God rest him,' Nanny had told Ruth, 'sent him that from America when he was born. Mike was a policeman in Los Angeles.'

Mike was also the tiger's name. From the moment he first laid eyes on him, when he was hardly more than an infant, Simon had fallen in love with Tiger Mike. Nanny had suggested that they take him home to the city, but Ruth and Phil preferred to leave him here so that Simon could play with him when he was down.

Now whenever Simon arrived at Nanny's, one of the first things that he always did was search out Tiger Mike. For as long as Simon was in the house the two were inseparable, and if Phil and Ruth took Simon on daytrips anywhere then Mike had to come too. Before going back to the city Simon would have a farewell chat with his friend, then put Tiger Mike back in his box with the other toys until next time. Simon never asked to take him home; the one time that Ruth asked whether he'd like to, Simon said no.

'Tiger Mike lives with Nanny,' he'd said. 'He minds her.'

Tiger Mike and Simon hadn't seen each other for over a month now, so Simon had a lot of things to report. He said nothing about the Pooshipaw, though. Partly he was trying to forget all that, and partly he was afraid of scaring Tiger Mike. Then again he felt maybe he himself had done something wrong, something that had made the Pooshipaw come; and he didn't want Tiger Mike to get a bad opinion of him.

Instead, after he'd introduced Saskia, Simon told Mike about life in the city. He told Mike about the time Daddy put his foot down the toilet while trying to open the jammed window in the bathroom, and how Eric cut his knee falling off the swing in the playground in playschool.

'There was blood,' Simon said to Tiger Mike. 'It was very red.'

Tiger Mike looked at him sympathetically. His great, half-shut, lemon-coloured eyes looked vaguely world-weary but very understanding. Saskia thought he looked half-drunk, but said nothing.

They sat on the round mat in the little bedroom and chatted. Saskia listened, charmed, and answered any questions that Mike, through Simon, asked her. Mike seemed very interested to hear that she had a beach at the bottom of her garden.

'Tiger Mike likes the sea,' Simon explained.

Ruth looked in to check that everything was all right, but Simon was too busy talking with Mike to notice, and Saskia was too busy listening to their conversation. Ruth watched the two children and the toy for a minute, then went away smiling to where Phil sat drinking a bottle of beer in the kitchen. Nanny always put a sixpack in the fridge when she heard they were coming.

'How are they doing?' Phil asked.

Ruth was still smiling. 'Simon's telling Tiger Mike about Eric's cut knee.'

'Eric?'

Ruth clicked her tongue at him. 'Honestly, Phil!' she said. 'Simon's friend in playschool!'

'Oh,' Phil said. 'That Eric!'

Ruth stood behind his chair and put her hands on his shoulders. Watching Simon talk to Tiger Mike had given her one of those warm moments that parents get.

'Oh Phil,' she said. 'It's terrible with the broken nights and all, but we've a wonderful son.'

Phil put a hand on one of hers. He leaned his head over onto her wrist. 'The best in the world,' he said. 'Wherever he gets it from.'

'I'm really glad we came down,' Ruth said. 'If only for Saskia's sake. She got a bit of a raw deal, arriving in the middle of all this.'

'I thought that too,' said Phil, who hadn't really, but felt he should have. 'Still, I think she'll like it down here. She prefers the country.'

Simon's Nanny arrived back a few minutes later. Ruth was still standing with her arms on Phil's shoulders. Simon's Nanny smiled at the picture they made. She was a parent too.

'I see the car is empty,' she said. 'Where's the little man?'

'Guess,' Ruth said.

Nanny grinned. 'Tiger Mike?'

'You got it,' Phil said. 'He's introducing Saskia.'

Nanny had a string shopping-bag full of packages. She was

putting it on the kitchen table when she stopped and looked around.

'What's that smell?' she said.

Ruth and Phil could smell nothing. 'Gas?' Phil suggested.

'The cooker wasn't on all day,' Nanny said. 'And it's not a gas smell.'

She looked around with a vague frown. 'I must be going queer in the head,' she said. 'For a minute I thought ...' She faltered.

'What?' her son asked.

Nanny shook her head. 'Nothing,' she said.

'I'll tell Simon you're back,' Ruth said.

She went out. Phil was looking at his mother. She was getting old, and sometimes he worried about her. 'Ma?' he said. 'Are you all right.'

'Of course I am. I just had a foolish notion.'

There was a loud cheer from the back room. Simon had obviously got the news.

'What sort of notion?' Phil asked.

Simon ran in waving Tiger Mike by one striped foot. His face was bright with happiness. Nanny's face lit up too, and she bent down and held out her arms. Simon ran right into them.

As Nanny clasped him Phil saw her face change. The brightness left it and a look of blank shock replaced it. She stood up with an effort, lifting Simon. She pulled her head back and stared at him. Then she leaned forward and sniffed loudly, again and again, smelling her grandson's skin.

Ruth stood frozen in the doorway, staring at her, with Saskia behind her. Phil looked over at Ruth and then back at his mother. Nanny was looking from one of them to the other with that same shocked look on her face.

'What's wrong, Ma?' he said.

Saskia stared at the old woman. She'd never seen anyone look so frightened. Nanny put Simon down.

'Ma?' Phil said. He sounded frightened. 'Mammy?'

The old woman stood up slowly and looked at him. Her face was white. She raised a shaking hand and pointed at Simon, who was talking to Mike about snails.

'That child,' she said, 'that child stinks.'

Ruth made a little noise of protest, but Saskia knew immediately that Phil's mother wasn't talking about dirt.

'You can't smell it, can you?' Nanny said. 'None of you.'

Then Saskia remembered the odd smell she'd seemed to smell in Simon's room that first night. She'd caught the same scent once or twice since, on the nights he'd had the dreams. It was a nasty smell that faded almost instantly, a smell so faint anyway that it was hardly there at all – the ghost of a smell, if there was such a thing. Even the memory of it seemed somehow hard to hold on to: every time the smell went she'd forget about it till the next night she smelled it.

'He had his bath last night,' Ruth said. There was a hint of annoyance in her voice, but mostly she sounded afraid. What was wrong with Phil's mother?

'No, no, no,' Nanny said. 'You don't understand. The child stinks of ...'

She hesitated. She seemed almost unwilling to finish the sentence. When she did, she whispered.

'He stinks,' she said, 'of Pooshipaw.'

BIRDIE MURRAY

'I'm going to feel ridiculous,' Ruth said. 'I know I am. I feel ridiculous already.'

'Me too,' said Phil. 'Completely ridiculous. But ...' He stopped and looked at her helplessly. Ruth nodded.

'Yes,' she said. 'But, Phil?'

He looked at her.

'Your mother really frightened me,' Ruth said.

'Yes. She frightened me as well.'

'Do you swear that you never mentioned the dreams to her?'

'Of course I didn't! When would I mention them? You were there any time I talked to her on the phone.'

'Then how did she know about the Pooshipaw? It was the first thing she said.'

Uncle Phil said nothing for a while. 'If I had an answer for that,' he said then, 'I wouldn't be doing this.'

It was later the same night. They were still in the kitchen. They were waiting for Simon's Nanny again. She'd gone to Birdie Murray's. Saskia could think of nothing to say to ease her aunt and uncle's worries. She'd found Simon's Nanny's behaviour pretty scary herself.

'She knew so much,' Ruth said. 'Too much. I'm out of my depth here, Phil.'

Simon was asleep. They'd left his door open a little so that they'd hear if he woke up, but his Nanny had assured them that he wouldn't.

'Or at least if he do,' she said, 'it'll be from an honest bad dream.'

She'd recovered quickly from her shock, almost forcing herself to be calm. You could see the effort it took. Then she'd quizzed Phil and Ruth, with a surprising sternness, about recent changes in Simon's life. Her mention of Pooshipaws had filled both of them with questions, but Simon's Nanny had refused to answer any of them until she'd had hers answered. Even then she'd been evasive.

'When he's asleep,' she said, 'I'll go for Birdie Murray. She's knows about these things. She'll tell you what she can. But I'll tell you one thing now – no, I'll tell you two.'

She held up a finger. 'First,' she said, 'something evil is after that boy.'

The way she said the word 'evil' made the hairs on Saskia's neck stand up.

Simon's Nanny held up a second finger. 'Second,' she said, 'it's not going to get him.'

That was all she'd say. At first Ruth and Phil had tried to make a joke of the way she was going on, but they didn't fool even themselves. Simon's Nanny had frightened them all badly. It wasn't even that she'd talked about the Pooshipaw; it was how frightened she'd seemed when she'd mentioned the name.

As soon as Simon went to bed his Nanny put her coat on.

'Ma,' Phil said, 'at least let me drive you.'

'No,' Nanny said. 'Stay with your wife. There's ways of doing these things.'

She was gone for nearly an hour. When she came back Birdie Murray was with her, a small, upright, bone-thin woman dressed entirely in black. Even Saskia felt nervous when Birdie walked into the room.

She knew that Birdie was ninety-five, but she'd never have guessed it. In some ways Birdie Murray didn't look any age at all. She looked like nothing from the modern world. Her face was sharp, unlined, and as blank as a stone. There were still dark streaks in her white hair. It was tied back in a tight bun and topped with a small dark straw hat. She had heavy-lidded eyes without expression. The whites of the eyes were yellowish. They reminded Saskia of something. It took her a while to think what. Yes! Birdie's eyes were a bit like Tiger Mike's – heavy-lidded and half-closed. But there was nothing sleepy or drunk about them at all.

Saskia kept thinking of that little resemblance to Mike. It made the old woman less scary. There was an air off her otherwise that didn't seem quite human. She had a terrible stillness about her, like a tree or a stone.

'God bless all here,' Birdie Murray said when she came in. She had a voice so hollow that it sounded like it came from underground. She stood just inside the door, looking around. After a while she began to sniff the air. Again Saskia felt the hair pricking up on her neck. She thought of that odd, nameless smell. As the thought went through Saskia's mind Birdie Murray turned her head and looked at her. Saskia thought she saw the old woman give a small nod, a movement so tiny that she couldn't be sure it was a movement at all.

'Can I get you a cup of tea, Mrs Murray?' Phil asked.

'No,' Birdie Murray said dismissively. She turned to Nanny. 'Where's the babby?' she asked.

'This way,' Nanny said. She left the room. Birdie Murray followed her.

Ruth looked at Uncle Phil. 'Phil ...' she said urgently. They both jumped out of their chairs and followed the two old women. For a moment Saskia was torn between curiosity and nervousness, then she followed too.

When they got to Simon's room Birdie Murray was leaning over Simon in the bed with her face pressed to his body. The blankets had been pulled down. Birdie was inhaling deeply, smelling the boy. She stood up and looked at Nanny.

'I was right?' Nanny said softly.

Birdie Murray nodded. 'You couldn't miss it,' she said.

'Please,' Ruth said. 'Shouldn't we talk outside? He'll wake up.'

Birdie turned and grinned at her, and Saskia saw that her teeth were more yellow than her eyes. There was no humour at all in her grin.

'He won't wake up,' she stated with an absolute certainty. She reached into her pocket and took out a small jar. The jar was half full of a dark powder. Birdie Murray unscrewed the lid and tipped a good pinch of the powder into the palm of one hand. Then she handed the jar and the lid to Nanny.

'Close that,' she said. 'Don't get any on you.'

'What's that stuff?' Phil asked her suspiciously. 'What are you going to do with it?'

Birdie Murray looked at him with her yellow eyes.

'If you knew what was in it, you wouldn't want me to use it,' she said. 'And if I don't use it you'll be sorry. As for what I'm going to do with it ...'

She turned and spat into her open palm, then rubbed the spit and powder together with her finger till they formed a dark paste. She scooped some of this up with two fingers of the mixing hand and bent over Simon.

Ruth was afraid. She'd never believed in anything super-natural, but this episode was frightening her. She watched uneasily as the small, dark, ancient woman bent over her child.

'Phil?' she said.

'Mrs Murray?' Phil said. 'You have to tell us ...'

'What I *have* to tell you is nothing,' Birdie Murray said without looking up. 'What I *will* tell you is what you can understand. But I'll tell you that after. The child comes first.'

'Is it far gone, Birdie?' Nanny asked.

Birdie Murray paused with her hand over Simon's forehead. 'Far enough,' she said. 'He'd have been gone in another month.'

She turned and looked at Simon's parents. 'A mystery death,' she said matter-of-factly. 'That's what it would have been called. Most child deaths are real enough, God help us, but this would have been another thing altogether.'

Saskia heard her aunt Ruth give a tiny whimper. Birdie Murray bent and rubbed the dark paste on Simon's forehead. She put her hand carefully inside the neck of his pyjamas and rubbed more on his chest. Then she stood up and looked straight at Ruth.

'This is superstition,' she said. There was no emotion in her voice. 'This is ould rubbish.'

Saskia saw Ruth blush. Ruth had used those very words tonight; but Birdie Murray hadn't been there when she'd used them.

Birdie pointed a long, stained finger at their son. 'Watch,' she said.

As they all watched, Simon's face seemed to change. It turned blotchy and then pale, and then it began to glow with an unhealthy, greenish light that seemed to be coming from under the skin.

Saskia grew cold. The whole figure of Simon was changing as it lay in the bed. It seemed to be slowly shrinking. Then the face collapsed in on itself. The pyjamas hung loose on a shrivelled, monkey-like figure. It looked less like a child than a little mummy. The paste on the mummy's forehead began to give off wisps of pale blue smoke. More smoke curled from the neck of its pyjamas.

Beside her Saskia heard Ruth make a strangled noise in her throat. It sounded like somebody who was trying to scream, but couldn't. Then, even as they watched, the face on the pillow blurred. For long seconds they couldn't make out its features at all. Then the blurring cleared, and Simon, unchanged, lay peacefully sleeping there. The dark smear of paste on his forehead was gone. His face glowed with nothing more than health.

'For the love of God!' Phil whispered. 'What was that?'

'The second part,' Birdie Murray said, 'was exactly that: for the love of God. The first part was another thing entirely. You'd never have seen that part; when you found the boy the next day he'd have looked more or less the way he do now. Except that he's breathing now, and except that it's really him.'

She looked at Simon with quite a different look now. Her eyes were actually fond.

'Do you know, May,' she said to Nanny, 'he's the spit and image of your Danny, God rest his soul, when he was a babby.' She looked at Phil. 'I minded your Da, you know,' she said. 'When he was a babby. Your son is the spit of him. You were always more like your mother's people.'

Saskia gasped. She was still looking at Simon. He'd opened his eyes but he was still half-asleep. Birdie Murray smiled down at him.

'Want a dummy,' Simon said sleepily.

Birdie bent and picked up one of the soothers lying beside him. She put it in his hand.

58

'Sleep sound, *a leanaveen*,' she said gently. 'We'll sort you out.'

Simon smiled and shook his head. 'No Pooshipaw now,' he said.

'Yerra child,' said Birdie Murray – she was almost whispering – 'sure we ates Pooshipaws for our breakfast. It's what gives us the yalla teeth.'

Simon grinned at her. Birdie looked at the others and nodded towards the door. Then she pulled the blanket up and tucked Simon in. He was asleep before they left the room.

IN THE KITCHEN

Saskia and the four adults sat around the kitchen table. They were all silent for a long time. Phil and Ruth were shaking. Finally Phil pulled himself together enough to offer Birdie Murray a cup of tea again.

'No,' she said. 'I don't ate nor drink. It's bad for me.'

Shocked as she was, Ruth thought she must have misheard. 'You mean you don't eat or drink anything?' she asked.

'No.'

'But what do you live on?'

Birdie Murray looked at her with no expression. 'On me pinshin,' she said.

'Your pension ...' said Phil.

Ruth looked from Birdie's blank face to her mother-in-law's. 'Will one of you tell us what's going on?' she asked. 'Please?'

'Your child is being got at be a Pooshipaw,' Birdie Murray said.

'But that's nonsense!' Phil said.

Birdie shrugged one shoulder. 'I can tell you he've the 'flu if it'll make you feel better about it,' she said. 'But he's still being got at be a Pooshipaw.'

'And what's a Pooshipaw?'

Birdie Murray spread her wrinkled hands flat on the table in front of her and looked at them in silence for a while. She frowned. 'It's a class of a creature,' she said then. 'A creature of evil. It's set on a child and it fastens on them. It hants them, you'd say.'

'Haunts them?' echoed Phil. 'But what does it look like?'

'To you? Nothing. You don't have eyes to see it. To Simon it probably looks like an animal. Or a mixture of animals. It makes up ... pictures. From the child's head. From the things the child's after seeing. But it'll be twisted in some way, I know that much.'

'Twisted?'

'Aye, twisted. Inside and out. Its heart will be where its liver should be, or its lungs will be in its head. It'll have two left hands, maybe, or two right ones, though that's less common. Or its head will be on backwards. I met one one time that had a foot instead of a head. That one was useless, of course.'

'Useless?' Phil frowned, perplexed.

'Yerra, man, sure its head was where its foot should be! It had to stand on its hands just to see where it was going.' She spoke matter-of-factly, but saw the widening eyes of Phil, Ruth and Saskia.

'A Pooshipaw is an unnatural thing,' she said. 'It's not right for people to make creatures, and so it's not permitted that they should make them true. So there's always something odd about them. Now this Pooshipaw, he smells like a left-hander, but I can't be sure till I see him.'

'Till you see him,' said Phil flatly.

Birdie Murray looked around her theatrically. 'I declare to God, May,' she said to Simon's Nanny, 'but you're after getting an awful echo in here.'

'I thought,' Ruth said, 'you said adults couldn't see them.'

'I said no such thing. I said *youse* couldn't see them. Sure youse couldn't even smell this one.'

'Phil's mother could. Could she see him too?'

'May? No. She's too nice.'

'Are you not nice, then, Mrs Murray?' Saskia asked.

Birdie Murray fixed her with a yellow stare. 'I am ...' she said, 'and I amn't.'

'You say this ... Pooshipaw causes death?' Phil said.

'I said it caused things that gets called death. Yerra, 'tis hard to put in words. The Pooshipaw takes the child away, do you see. It hollows it out, then it takes it away, and it leaves something else there instead.'

Phil struggled with half-remembered folk stories he'd heard as a child and had put out of his mind long ago.

'Some kind of changeling?' he suggested.

'Not the way you mean, but it leaves an exchange – a dead shell that looks like the child.'

Saskia was watching Ruth. She saw a host of contradictory emotions flit across her aunt's face. She was thinking, Saskia knew, that she didn't believe in this nonsense. But it was hard after what she'd seen in Simon's bedroom, whatever it had been.

'How ... how close was Simon?' Ruth made herself ask. 'What did you say – a month?'

Birdie Murray shrugged one shoulder. She was still looking at her hands. She'd washed them for a long time before sitting down.

'A month ...' she said, 'six weeks. It depends. You took the child away. The Pooshipaw will have to start again when you go back. It won't like that.'

'Let me get this straight,' Phil said. 'An evil creature is after our son ...'

'No. A creature of evil.'

'What's the difference?'

'The creature is not evil in itself. No creature is – or nearly none. God knows, Pooshipaws are grumpy at the best of times, but they can be good company if you know how to deal with them.'

Phil was looking at her blankly. Birdie Murray saw his look.

'Nothing,' she said, 'is simple, Philip, except to lazy minds.'

Saskia had often heard her father say something very similar. She wondered what he'd make of Birdie Murray. She was the sort of odd character he always said had made him fall in love with Ireland when he'd first come here. Then she wondered what Birdie Murray would make of her father. An artist would seem as weird to her, perhaps, as she would to him.

As though she'd heard Saskia's thoughts, the old woman's head swivelled towards her. Saskia found herself looking into the yellow eyes like Tiger Mike's. They seemed to have a great depth to them, those yellow eyes.

'There's arts, young lady,' Birdie Murray said primly, 'and there's arts. And all true artists respects one another.'

Saskia stared at her wide-eyed.

'Mrs Murray,' Phil said, 'you make this ... Pooshipaw sound evil enough to me.'

Birdie Murray shrugged. "'Tis lots that you know about evil, I dare say,' she said. 'Tell me this: is a fire good on a winter's night?'

Phil was puzzled. 'Of course,' he said.

'And if it's your house that's afire?'

'Well ... I mean ...'

'A man with a hatchet chops wood,' Birdie Murray said. 'He gives you the wood for your fireplace. The next day he takes the same hatchet and puts it through your window. Is the hatchet good or bad? Well?'

'In that case,' Phil said impatiently, 'the good or bad is in the man, not the hatchet.'

'There you are, then. A Pooshipaw is a Pooshipaw, like a hatchet is a hatchet. The good or bad is in the one that sets him on the child.'

'It's hard to believe the thing exists,' Phil said. 'It's even harder to think there's a person who ... set it on our son.'

'A sort of a person,' Birdie Murray corrected him.

'But who? Why? How?'

She looked up at him. 'Your Ma says you bought the child a bed,' she said. 'It wasn't a new bed.'

'Why no. We bought it secondhand. But ...' He stopped. 'No,' he said. 'I can't credit this. You're telling me some kind of evil witch set a monster on my child?'

Birdie Murray considered. 'Aye,' she said. 'Give or take a word or two, that's about the size of it.'

'But that's insane!'

Birdie Murray shrugged again. 'I can't help that,' she said. 'It's what happened.'

Ruth knew exactly how her husband felt, but she didn't know any more how she felt herself. Simon's Nanny had mentioned the word Pooshipaw straight away. And certainly something very strange had happened in that bedroom. She felt in her heart that the something, whatever it was, had been a good thing. She'd felt that with some basic part of her. And she knew it wasn't over.

'What do we do next?' she asked Birdie Murray, interrupting her husband's protestations.

The old woman looked at her with those blank, heavy eyes. 'That Pooshipaw is in that bed,' she said. 'He can't venture far from it, but he's there.'

'Right,' Phil said. 'We'll dump the bed as soon as we get home. Will that do the job?'

'Grand! But what about the man that set the Pooshipaw on him? He might decide to try another way. He's after putting time in on this job. And your son won't be the first, you know. Not be a long chalk.'

'But what is all this? Some kind of cult? You say they take children. Take them to where?'

Birdie Murray shook her head again.

'That's not your business,' she said. 'Be glad of that. This is an ould fight. It started before your time, and it will go on after your time. Aye, and after Simon's time, and after his grandchilders'. What we have to do now is do the things that have to be done, no more and no less.'

'And they are?'

'Simon have to be protected. The Pooshipaw have to be destroyed. The man who set him on Simon have to be dealt with.'

Phil snorted. 'Dealt with? You mean I should phone the police and tell them some man sold me a bed with a monster in it?'

For the first time since she'd arrived the ghost of something like a genuine smile crossed Birdie Murray's face. 'Begob, but

I'd like to hear what they said to that, right enough,' she said. 'But no, there's ways of dealing with all of these things. There's more nor one kind of criminal, you know. And there's more nor one kind of police.'

'I suspect,' Phil said, 'that you're referring to yourself.'

'I am.'

'With all due respect, Mrs Murray, you're ninety-five years old. I mean, you seem to know something about what's going on, but you're not physically strong.'

The ghost of a smile disappeared from Birdie Murray's face. She stared into Phil's eyes. He stopped talking, his mouth open. Saskia felt the room grow cold.

'Childeen,' Birdie said to Phil, 'don't you rouse me. I'm a divil when I'm roused. It's ould dogs for the hard roads, and pups for paths. And I'm an ould dog, Philip, and this is a hard road. I'm going to get that Pooshipaw, and I'm going to get the one as sent him. I'm not asking you for your help or your permission.'

'Why are you so set on this, Mrs Murray?' Ruth asked. 'You sound like you take it all personally.'

Birdie Murray turned and smiled a definite smile at her. Only one side of her mouth smiled, but it was a definite smile. When she took her eyes off Phil he sat back in his chair with a dazed look on his face.

'I do take it personal,' Birdie said to Ruth. 'I takes it very personal. It's me job. And I lives for me work.'

A HOLIDAY

That night they all expected to be sleepless. But before leaving Birdie Murray assured them this wouldn't be so.

'You'll all rest now,' she said. 'You'll stay calm.'

It sounded more like an order than anything else. But sure enough all of them felt themselves start to relax even as she spoke. After Birdie left, Nanny made tea. After the tea they all wanted to discuss the night's weird events, but the four of them found that actually they were unbearably tired.

'That woman did something to us,' Phil complained.

'She did something to Simon,' Ruth said. 'Whatever it was.'

'It had a good feeling to it,' Saskia said with certainty. From the way that Aunt Ruth looked at her she knew she'd felt it too. But Uncle Phil seemed inclined to quibble through his yawns.

'Oh shut up, Phil,' Ruth said.

Simon's Nanny grinned. She seemed quite calm, almost cheerful now that Birdie was involved.

Within half an hour they'd all gone to bed. In the room she was sharing with Simon, Saskia lay for a minute or two looking over at him as he slept in the other bed. She felt certain that he was safe, but she still didn't understand what it was he might be safe from. Safe from his dreams. In an odd way she found it exciting to imagine having dreams you might need to be saved from. No fear of that with her own dreams, more's the pity. Then she fell asleep.

Simon slept peacefully through the night. He was still asleep next day when Saskia woke up. It was almost ten o'clock. She put on her dressing-gown and tiptoed from the room. She found Ruth and Phil in the kitchen having breakfast. They weren't long up themselves, but already they were deep in discussion of the night before. They greeted Saskia only briefly before returning to their talk.

'That woman did something to all of us,' Phil said.

'You mean she put a spell on us or something?' Saskia asked.

'I don't know. It sounds stupid when you put it like that.'

'The whole thing sounds stupid,' Ruth said. 'But I believe it, I think. At least I believe I saw something very strange in that bedroom last night.'

'Maybe she hypnotised us,' Phil said.

'I'll tell you, Phil,' Ruth said. 'I hardly care at this point. All I know is that I had the best night's rest last night that I've had in a month. And I still feel good today. I don't mean just rested, either. I feel good that Birdie Murray is involved. I know I laughed at her yesterday, but I hadn't seen her in action then.'

'She's a very impressive woman,' Saskia said through a mouthful of cornflakes.

'Yes,' Ruth said. 'That's it exactly. She's impressive. I feel crazy even saying it, but I feel confidence in Birdie Murray. She's so ... reassuring, in a way.'

'Aye,' her husband said. 'A damned peculiar way.'

They'd both half-expected the situation to look different in the cold light of day. Simon's dreams had worried them, of course, but surely they were really only dreams. Two superstitious old women had said they were something more sinister, but that was impossible.

That was how they'd expected to feel, but in fact they didn't feel like that at all. They felt their son was being haunted by a Pooshipaw, even though they still had no clear idea what a Pooshipaw was. Nanny wouldn't discuss it.

'It's in Birdie's hands now,' she said when they mentioned the matter.

And still they didn't panic, though they felt they had every right to. Whenever they worried they thought of Birdie Murray, and how sure of herself she seemed, and then they felt better about the whole thing.

The week of the holiday passed in this haze of reassurance. It was the most relaxed week that Phil and Ruth had had since the coming of the bad dreams. More than that, it was the most relaxed they'd had in years. They couldn't understand it, but they soon stopped trying. They were having too good a time.

Simon helped to distract them from possible worries. For the whole week he was in something very like heaven. He loved the constant presence of Saskia and his Nanny, and the daily trips into the village where he was much admired. He loved every single instant of his being there, and slept through the nights like a log, worn out by mad runs through green fields with his cousin. Even in his sleep he seemed to glow with health and happiness.

Saskia had a great time too. The countryside here was green and lush and tamed, very different from what she was used to; but any place with people like Birdie Murray in it, she figured, didn't need much more in the way of wildness.

The old woman fascinated her. There was something of the same ancient air about her that Saskia felt sometimes from the ocean near her home. Sometimes in winter, when the storms came roaring mad off the Atlantic, Saskia would wrap up and venture out into the lashing rain to scream at the sky.

You could put all your anger into the screams, all your annoyance and frustration, and the terrible power of the wind and the rain and the waves would take them up and blow them all away. She felt Birdie Murray had in her something of that same strength, not the strength of a muscle or a machine but the power of a mountain or a sea.

The sea here, in summer at least, was nothing at all like the ocean she knew best. It was perfect for daytrips, though. During that week they made two trips to the beach. Simon approved of the sea.

'Sea,' he said, 'I like you!' And the waves hissed their gratitude on the warm sand of the beach, and Saskia interpreted their words for Simon. Since she lived by the sea, she told him, she'd learned its language. This made perfect sense to Simon, who thought it was a handy skill to have.

They brought picnic lunches on the daytrips, and on the second trip Nanny came along. Simon took her along the beach with a bucket and spade that they'd bought in the village, and showed her how to make sandcastles. She was suitably impressed.

When they got back to the house that time Birdie Murray was waiting for them. Her tall old bicycle – the high nellie, as Nanny called it – was standing propped against the wall.

'I needs something of Simon's,' she said. 'Have he any toys here with him?'

'Only my old ones that he plays with,' Phil said.

'I needs a toy he's friendly with,' Birdie said. 'Is there any he specially likes?'

'Tiger Mike,' said Ruth and Phil at the same time.

Birdie Murray nodded. 'That's the yoke your uncle Mike sent from America,' she said to Phil.

'It is.'

'Good,' Birdie Murray said. 'That's perfect.'

She turned to Simon, who was delighted to see her. 'Your friend Mike is coming for a visit to my house,' she said. 'Is that all right?'

'Simon will go too,' Simon said.

Birdie Murray looked at his parents. 'That would be useful,' she said. 'I'll have them back by seven.'

Ruth and Phil looked at each other, briefly concerned. There was a dry clucking sound from Birdie, who'd seen the glance they'd exchanged. It took them a while to realise she was laughing at them.

'Nothing will happen to him,' she said. 'Nothing bad, anyhow.' She turned to Simon. 'You go and get this Tiger Mike,' she said. When Simon went she turned to Phil. 'I hope this tiger is house-trained,' she said. 'It's more nor your uncle Mike ever was. Though he had a terrible end, God help us.'

'But didn't Mike die in his sleep?' Phil asked.

'I don't mean the way he died,' Birdie Murray said. 'I mean that he joined the police over in America. And him such a nice chap and he young.'

Simon came out of the house swinging Tiger Mike by the tail. Tiger Mike didn't seem to mind. He never did.

'Is Saskia coming?' Simon said.

Birdie Murray looked calculatingly at Saskia. 'The artist's daughter,' she said. 'Do you want to involve yourself in this, girl?'

Saskia had been hoping for a chance to talk to Birdie Murray alone. During the holiday she'd been doing a lot of thinking. But now for a moment she didn't know what to say. Something in the old woman's tone suggested somehow that she was referring to more than just going to her house. But Saskia's hesitation lasted no more than a few seconds, and she tried not to seem too keen when she answered.

'If Simon wants,' she said.

Birdie looked at her. 'Simon wants,' she said. 'And I wants too, for that matter. But you have to want it as well.'

There was an odd sort of look in her eyes as she spoke. It was as though she'd issued a challenge of some kind to Saskia and was curious to see the girl's reaction. That was the sort of thing that would have made Saskia go, even if she hadn't been dying to go along anyway.

'I'm on,' she said.

Birdie Murray nodded, looking satisfied.

'Will I drive you?' Phil said.

'Yerra, man,' Birdie Murray said, 'youse are all mad on yer cars nowadays.'

She picked Simon up and swung him into the big wicker basket in front of the handlebars on her bike. Simon thought this was wonderful. Only his head and shoulders showed above the rim of the basket. He giggled and waved at his parents.

Birdie Murray climbed up on the bike. 'Can you get on the carrier?' she asked Saskia. Saskia was well used to high bikes from being in Holland, where her Dutch grandmother rode a bike hardly smaller than Birdie's. She clambered up and sat astride the carrier, her face inches from Birdie Murray's straight, black-clad back. She smelled the clean, starchy smell of the old woman's coal-black shirt.

'See you la-ter,' Simon cooed to his parents.

Birdie Murray rode out of the yard without looking back. Ruth and Phil stood looking after her.

'I wonder what she's doing,' Phil said.

'I don't know,' said Ruth. 'But she obviously does. Did you see the way she picked Simon up? She doesn't move like a woman of ninety-five.'

'She doesn't do anything like anyone, as far as I can see,' Phil said. 'You know, there's something about Birdie that's been bothering me.'

'Apart from the obvious, you mean.'

'Yes, apart from her contempt and her weirdness and her bossiness. I keep thinking I've seen her before.'

'But you have. Lots of times.'

'No, I mean lately.' He shook his head. 'Never mind,' he said. 'It'll come to me.'

AT BIRDIE'S

Birdie Murray's house was up a narrow, climbing lane. She cycled up the slope with no sign of being bothered by her extra burden. They stopped at a small iron gate with two white stone pillars. Saskia jumped off the carrier and took Simon from the basket, while Birdie kept the high old bike upright. Simon held on tightly to Tiger Mike.

'So,' Birdie Murray said, 'here we are.' She reached out and laid a hand on Saskia's shoulder. When Saskia turned to face her she found the old eyes looking into her own with a terrible intensity. 'You'll say nothing of anything you see here,' she said.

Saskia had been hoping to see something odd. 'I promise,' she said.

Birdie Murray clucked. 'I wasn't asking for a promise,' she said. 'I was just telling you what's going to happen. You'll say nothing of anything you see, and I'll say nothing of anything I hear.'

A bantam cock was standing on one of the gate-pillars. It clucked and glowered beadily at them.

'Watch it, Chick,' said Birdie warningly to the bird. She turned to Saskia. 'Ould Chick there,' she said, 'don't like childer so much. But don't pay him any mind.'

As they went in Saskia held the gate open so Birdie could wheel in her bike. She kept one wary eye on the bantam, who eyed her just as warily. It was the first time that Saskia had ever seen a chicken looking sulky.

Once she had a chance to look around, though, Saskia forgot about the bird.

'Oh, this is lovely!' she said.

The hedges in the lane were high, and she'd seen nothing of Birdie's house till they were inside them. Now she saw a plain, snug, whitewashed cottage standing in a steeply sloping field of maybe a couple of acres in size. Around the door of the cottage a half-dozen bantam hens picked idly at the ground. The ridge of the low roof seemed hardly taller than Birdie herself. There were neatly-kept vegetable and herb gardens under the cottage windows, and a gravel path led to the front door. Otherwise, apart from a little henhouse and a clothesline, the field looked left to nature. From somewhere down the slope Saskia could hear water running with an almost musical sound.

'Have you got your very own river, Mrs Murray?' she asked.

'Aye,' Birdie said. 'It's handy betimes.'

A fat little donkey and an aged-looking black cow had been browsing companionably in a corner of the field near the house. When they saw Birdie they came trotting over. Simon gurgled in delight as the donkey lowered its head to look into his eyes. Birdie scratched the cow between its horns.

'This is Ned and Nora,' Birdie said. 'Ned is the ass. Ned, Nora, this is Saskia and Simon. Simon is the chap.'

Nora's adoring eyes strayed momentarily from Birdie to take in the children. Simon was still gurgling at Ned, who stared at him with great seriousness and nodded now and then.

'Go on now, the pair of youse,' Birdie said. 'We've business to do.'

For a moment Saskia wasn't sure which pair she meant, but then Ned and Nora turned obediently and trotted off. Ned looked longingly over his shoulder at Simon.

'Ned, now,' Birdie said, 'have a great liking for childer. Him and Simon can have a chat after.'

She led the way up the little path to her front door. The hens made way for them grudgingly until Simon grabbed the tail of one of them. Then the birds scattered with much outraged clucking and scurried towards the henhouse. Simon was left holding a tailfeather. Chick, the rooster, crowed sourly at them from the gate-pillar. Birdie turned to him with a scowl.

'Shut it, you,' she said.

'You don't seem to like your chickens much,' Saskia said.

'Yerra, I do and I don't,' Birdie said. She stood her high bike against the wall by the door.

'Why do you keep them, then?' Saskia asked. 'It can't be for the eggs – you told Phil and Ruth you don't eat.'

Birdie paused with her hand on the latch. 'Are you giving me cheek, young one?' she asked.

'I suppose so,' Saskia said. 'But only a tiny bit.'

The yellow teeth grinned at her briefly. 'I likes a bit of spirit in a person,' Birdie said. 'That Daddy of Simon's is after losing a lot of it since he went to the city.'

She turned and looked after the scurrying bantams. 'I do like,' she said then, 'the sound of hens in the mornings. And sometimes of an evening in the summer, when they're in the henhouse, I sits outside it and listens to the little clucks. It's a lovely soft sound.'

She lifted the latch on the door and led the way in. Saskia had been wondering what to expect of Birdie's house. It seemed natural, somehow, that the home of a witch would be full of things for making spells. But Birdie's cottage was just old-fashioned. The furniture was plain, the walls white-washed. On one wall hung a picture of two popes and an American president. You could see the same picture in many old Irish houses.

'I hope you're not disappointed,' Birdie said. Again Saskia had the feeling that the old woman had read her thoughts.

'I didn't know what to expect,' she admitted. 'Stuff for making potions, I suppose – like that stuff you used on Simon.'

Birdie Murray actually cackled. 'Yerra,' she said, 'that was only an ould bit of ashes out of the fire.'

She noticed the surprise on Saskia's face. 'People likes a bit of a show,' she said. 'It helps them to believe. Grown-up people haves trouble believing things sometimes.'

She looked almost embarrassed, and Saskia couldn't help laughing. Birdie made a face, but she looked quite pleased, really. Then Saskia remembered that, whatever had been in the powder, something genuinely strange had happened in Simon's room that night. She stopped laughing.

'Aye,' Birdie said. 'That was no laughing matter.'

Simon and Tiger Mike had been walking around looking at everything in the room. Now Birdie asked Simon for Tiger

Mike. She held the animal close to her face and looked into its fixed, friendly eyes. She tut-tutted.

'The dear knows what you'll be like, boyo,' she muttered.

'What do you need him for?' Saskia asked.

'I think nowadays it's called "muscle",' Birdie Murray said. 'And he'll be a distraction.'

None of this made any sense to Saskia. 'What are you going to do with him?' she asked.

Birdie thought for a bit. 'Do you know,' she said, 'I couldn't tell you exactly.'

'Would I not understand?'

Birdie scratched the back of her head. 'I don't even understand it all meself,' she said. 'And the bits that I do understand don't fit into words. They're slippery things, words.'

She held the stuffed tiger out towards Saskia so that its yellow eyes were looking at her. 'I'm going to give this fella his dreams,' she said.

'But toys don't dream, do they?'

'Sure everything dreams, childeen. Everything dreams grand dreams.'

Saskia was painfully reminded again of her own dull dream-world.

'Not everything remembers its grand dreams,' Birdie Murray said, again as though answering her thoughts. 'But that don't mean they're not there. Even Pooshipaws dreams, though they don't know it.'

'And what do they dream of?'

'More,' Birdie Murray said.

'More?'

'More. They lives terrible small lives, you know. Cut off. Stunted. Misshapen. So they dreams of having their odd bits

76

untwisted. They dreams of all the things we takes for granted. They dreams of more.'

Saskia didn't quite understand but she let it pass. 'And yourself, Mrs Murray,' she asked. 'Do you dream?'

'Oh I do, bedad.'

'Grand dreams?'

'Oh, grand dreams altogether'

'And what grand dreams do you have?'

'I dreams of a rest, child,' Birdie Murray said. 'A good long rest. I'm due one soon.'

She turned suddenly and put Tiger Mike down carefully in the middle of the deal table that stood by her window. Then she rummaged in a dresser drawer and took out four little bowls. She handed one of them to Saskia.

'Go outside,' she said, 'and put four good pinches of dirt in that for me.'

'Dirt,' said Saskia.

'Aye, dirt. Earth. Dust from there where the hens were picking. And just four, mind you. The size of the pinches don't matter, but there haves to be four.'

Saskia did as she was told. There was no sign outside now of the bantams. She saw the head of Chick, the cock, eyeing her from the small door of the henhouse, and guessed the birds were hiding till the visitors left.

When she went back inside she saw that Birdie Murray had put the other three bowls on the table around Tiger Mike. There was water in one of them now, and in another a thin red candle stood lighting. The third bowl was empty. Birdie Murray took the bowl of earth from Saskia and put it on the table too.

'Do you see that empty bowl?' Birdie Murray said. 'Just breathe in that for me, will you?'

Saskia stared at her in surprise. 'Breathe in it?' she asked.

'Aye. It'll spill, but it don't matter.'

Feeling foolish, Saskia did as she was bid. In spite of herself she watched to see whether anything would happen when she breathed into the empty bowl, but nothing did. It was just a bowl – a bowl of breath now, she supposed, feeling even more foolish.

'Is this just a bit of a show for me?' she asked. Birdie Murray hushed her with a look and leaned close.

'It's for the tiger,' she hissed, nodding secretively towards the table.

In spite of herself Saskia looked at Tiger Mike, but his face looked as blandly fixed as before. 'Oh,' she said. 'Right.'

Simon was standing by the bowl with the candle in it, staring at the flame. He told them fire was dangerous for little boys.

'Bedad, you're right, Simon,' Birdie said. 'But you'll be all right in my house. Fire is my special friend, and it don't hurt my other friends.'

She surveyed the arrangement on the table, then turned to Saskia.

'Right! Now,' she said, brisk and businesslike, 'I have a bit of a thing to do with Simon. You go outside and wait for us. We'll only be a minute.'

Saskia went outside and looked around. Evening was coming on. The cow and the donkey looked over when they saw her, but made no move to approach. The hens were still in the henhouse. Everything was very quiet.

Still feeling foolish, Saskia walked over and stood beside the shed and listened; but all she heard was Chick's complaining cluck. She was suddenly quite sad. She wanted very much to be part of this adventure, but there was obviously a lot of it she couldn't share. It wasn't really her adventure at all. She felt suddenly very alone, standing there in Birdie's yard, alone and lonely.

Ned and Nora were back in their corner browsing. The water in the unseen stream still chuckled, with a sound like music, over a stony bed. After a while Birdie and Simon came out of the house. Simon's eyes were wide, and he was wearing a big grin.

'It's nearly six o'clock,' Birdie said. 'We'll have to leave that tiger there for half an hour or so.' She turned to Simon. 'Why don't you go and chat with Ned?' she suggested.

Simon trotted off happily. The donkey had already started over. They met half way, and stood talking. The donkey did most of the listening.

'Well,' Birdie Murray said to Saskia. 'We'll have to wait here now. Do you want to ask me that thing?'

'Ask you what thing?'

'That thing that you wanted to ask me.'

Saskia looked at her. She felt suddenly embarrassed. What she'd meant to ask Birdie about was an idea she'd had about her Problem. It was a pretty mad idea, but then it was a pretty mad problem. And surely Birdie could help her if anyone could. But the Problem felt terribly personal and intimate, and – compared to Simon's danger – unimportant. She'd hoped that Birdie would somehow see what she wanted to say.

'You have to tell me,' Birdie Murray said gently. 'That makes it my business. Otherwise I'm only snooping, and I'm not let do that. These things haves rules, do you see. And after you ask me for something, I ask you for something. Tit for tat, like. And I have a thing to ask you, childeen, that might interest you an awful lot.'

'You really have something to ask me?' Saskia repeated. It seemed very unlikely somehow.

'Let's say I have a proposition to put to you. But you first. Ask me the thing.'

Saskia didn't know what to think. What could Birdie Murray need from her? She looked at this craggy old woman and wondered whether she could even express the Problem to her. But then again telling things to Birdie wouldn't be like telling them to anyone else. It would be like telling them to a rock, except that the rock might have some advice to give. Perhaps if she did it in a roundabout way, beginning near the end ...

'Mrs Murray,' she began, 'can you tell me some more about Pooshipaws?'

A slow grin, with a tiny hint of evil in it, spread across Birdie Murray's face. 'Pooshipaws?' she asked. 'And sure why would a nice girl like you want to know about Pooshipaws?'

'Well, I had this notion,' Saskia said, 'and I was just wondering how mad it was.'

Birdie Murray was looking at her mildly with that evil little grin on her face. Saskia took a deep breath.

'Well you see,' she said, 'it's like this ...'

And she told Birdie about the Problem, and they sat and talked of a great many things odd and ordinary. And in the course of their long conversation Birdie Murray too asked something, outlining the proposition she'd mentioned. And as Saskia sat and listened, and realised what was being asked of her, and how it sort-of connected with her own questions, she could feel her eyes getting wider and wider. After a while she was grinning herself, with a grin which – if she could have seen it – had its own little hint of evil in it; a hint of evil, and rather more than a hint of fear.

PART TWO

THE MAKING OF MAGIC

A HOUSEFUL OF FLEAS

They were back in Simon's Nanny's house by seven. They knocked on the door, and when Nanny opened it Simon was standing there grinning, with Tiger Mike in his arms and Saskia standing behind him. Birdie Murray had gone. Simon came in singing.

'It looks like you enjoyed yourself,' his Daddy said.

'Auntie Birdie's house is a mystery,' Simon said.

Phil laughed. 'That's the best I ever heard,' he said to Ruth. 'That's exactly what Birdie's house is – a mystery. What did you make of the place, Saskia?'

But Saskia was just standing there, smiling, with a strange light in her eyes and a glowing face.

'Saskia?' Phil said again.

'I thought it was a mystery too,' Saskia said dreamily, but she would say no more.

'Remember I told you we all thought Birdie was a witch?' Phil asked Ruth.

'But isn't that exactly what she is?' Ruth said.

'Go on with you,' Nanny corrected her. 'Birdie is a helpful woman, that's all.'

'Helpful?' Phil said. 'She's certainly that. But it depends what you mean by helpful.'

'What I mean by helpful,' Nanny said tartly, 'depends on what kind of trouble you have. And for the kind of trouble that you and Ruth have, Birdie is the best help you could get.'

It was true, Ruth knew. It went against everything she'd ever believed, but it was true. Her reason couldn't understand anything of what was going on, but then what was going on wasn't reasonable. From the moment Birdie Murray had walked in on that first evening, she'd known that this small, odd-looking woman knew exactly what she was doing. That was a comfort.

The holiday continued to pass in sunshine and pleasure. They saw no more of Birdie during the week, and if Phil and Ruth wondered about that then neither of them said anything. On several evenings Nanny hooshed them out of the house to the village pub, while she stayed and had long talks with Saskia. The two of them had taken to each other in a great way.

On their pub evenings, Ruth and Phil chatted to old men and joined in singsongs. They met old schoolfriends of Phil's who embarrassed him – and delighted Ruth – by recalling his youthful escapades. They never brought the car on these evening outings. When the pub closed they'd get a lift to Nanny's gate from someone or else stroll home arm-in-arm on the black, unlit road, giggling like kids and looking at the stars. On the whole they preferred to walk. Sometimes, walking home, they'd kiss like a pair of teenagers. Afterwards Ruth would giggle.

'I haven't heard you giggle in years,' Phil said to her one night.

'Neither have I,' she answered.

'I like it,' he said.

'So do I.'

Slowly though the days went, they did eventually all go, and then it was time to go home. Ruth and Phil had been warning Simon for two whole days, so that it wouldn't come as a nasty surprise to him. But he seemed well prepared.

'Tiger Mike,' he said firmly, 'is coming too. Auntie Birdie says.'

His parents had obviously wondered what happened when Tiger Mike and Simon were in Birdie's house, but they hadn't discussed it. Saskia said she'd seen nothing special happen, but whenever the subject came up she had an echo of that glow she'd worn when she'd come back. She'd certainly been different in some subtle way since the visit. She was obviously enjoying the holiday, and played as many mad games with Simon as before, but she got very thoughtful sometimes. She would sit looking off into the distance, as though gazing at something that no-one else could see. 'Dreamy,' Phil called it when discussing it with Ruth one night. It was partly her age, Ruth had said, but Phil wasn't so sure. Often in her dreamy moods Saskia tended to grin to herself in a way Phil found suspicious; but once or twice he'd caught her looking very pensive, nearly frightened. It had made him feel almost guilty at the way he and Ruth were enjoying themselves, even though he was certain that Birdie Murray had something to do with their own seeming inability to worry.

'Don't fret, Saskia,' he'd even said to her once. 'I'm certain it will all work out.'

She'd been sitting looking out the kitchen window at nothing in particular, with a serious look on her face that was a new thing there in his experience. At his words she'd turned to him, blinking.

'Phil,' she said, 'I didn't see you there. What did you say?'

'I said it will all work out.'

'It?'

'This ... Pooshipaw business. We have to trust Mrs Murray.' He'd found himself uneasy saying that.

'Oh,' Saskia had said. 'Yes. Yes, I'm sure it will. But we have to be strong, you know.'

Phil didn't like being told things like that by a twelve-year-old. If there was any reassuring to be done, he felt that he should be the one to do it. It had annoyed him for a while, but then the annoyance had just faded and he forgot it had existed. At any rate he'd certainly given up on getting any information from Saskia about the events at Birdie Murray's cottage. He'd taken a good long look at Tiger Mike, to see if he looked any different, but he'd seen nothing odd.

'If Birdie says Tiger Mike is coming,' he told Simon now, 'then he's coming.'

They'd decided to leave on the Saturday afternoon. Both Phil and Ruth were due back at work on Monday, and they wanted a full day at home before then to adjust. Even when your child is being got at by monsters, as Ruth said, you have to be practical.

On Saturday morning Ruth made a point of getting Nanny alone.

'I just wanted to tell you,' she said, 'that this was the best holiday I ever had. It really was. I never felt so relaxed in my whole life. And with all that's going on, I don't really understand why.'

Nanny took her by the hand, the first time that she'd ever done so.

'Because you're safe here,' she said. 'And because you're starting to know that I love all of you.'

They hugged for the first time in their lives. When Phil came into the kitchen with Saskia a few minutes later they were still standing there hugging.

'What's this?' he said.

'A man wouldn't understand,' his mother said. She went to

85

the cooker and put on the old-fashioned kettle.

'And a woman wouldn't ask,' Saskia said, leaving her uncle with the vague feeling that he was being ganged-up on.

'No sign of Birdie with last-minute instructions,' he said.

'Hush,' Nanny said. 'You're not gone yet.'

'She'll be here,' Saskia said with the sort of calm certainty Phil hated.

'I hope we can rely on her,' he said

'You get these people back home safe,' Nanny said. 'The rest will be taken care of.'

'I just wish I understood what Birdie was doing to fight this ... Pooshipaw,' Phil said. He still had trouble making himself say the word. He thought it sounded silly.

'If it works,' Nanny said, 'then there's no need for you to understand. So long as Birdie does.'

Then she told them one of her stories. It was a way she had, of commenting on one thing by telling a story about something else altogether. Her 'parables', Phil called them. He didn't mean any insult: he'd always found the stories had a point.

'When you were a babby,' Nanny said, 'myself and your father used to keep hens in the back yard. One time a rat got in and started killing the chickens. You wouldn't mind one or two that they'd take for food, but this rat used to kill half a dozen and leave them there. The hens went mad. They stopped laying altogether. One morning your Da heard them making noise and went out. The rat was in the henhouse. Your Da blocked the entrance with a bit of an ould board. He went and got Bob Daley. Can you recall Bob?'

'A little sallow man,' Phil said. 'He had an old terrier that went everywhere with him.'

'Aye, that was them. Bob was a comical man. That terrier

was the best ratter I ever seen in my life. Tinker, his name was. He was as cute as a christian. Anyhow, Bob and Tinker came. Your Da went ahead on to work. I was looking out the back window. Bob took the board off the henhouse door and then he came in and asked me for a cup of tea.

'"What about the rat, Bob?" says I. "Would you not do better to stay out and make sure of him?" Well, Bob looked at me all funny, like I was after saying something terrible. He pointed out the window at Tinker, sitting there beside the little hatch in the henhouse with his hackles up. "Sure I'd only get in his way, ma'am," says Bob. "I'm only the foreman. And a good foreman knows better nor to hinder a craftsman while he's working."'

Phil couldn't think of anything to say, so he said nothing. This was unusual for him.

They left in the afternoon. Nanny stood outside the house waving as they went. Phil, remembering Saskia's certainty that Birdie would come, felt a tiny bit smug. But as the car turned out on the roadway they saw Birdie Murray standing there stiffly, holding her high bike. She looked as though she'd been waiting for them.

Phil stopped the car and wound down his window.

'Were you calling to see us?' he asked.

'Amn't I seeing you now?' Birdie said. She leaned over and spoke in the window.

'Put him to bed tonight the way you always do,' she said. 'Nothing will happen. It will take a bit for the beast to get going again. It's like with a houseful of fleas.'

Phil looked blank. Birdie Murray sighed.

'If a house that have fleas is empty for a while,' she said, 'the fleas gets very quiet. They goes asleep. If you go into that house then nothing happens for a while. But as you moves around the house they feels the vibrations. They starts to stir. And sure the next thing you know you're being ate alive.'

Phil thought about that. 'You know,' he said, 'it's not so scary when you think of it as an infestation. Like fleas.'

'Good,' Birdie Murray said. 'You think of it like that, then.' She smiled at Simon, who was calling her from the back seat. 'The fun will start in earnest tomorrow night,' she said to Phil. 'I'll call on youse in the morning.'

'But we're going home now,' Phil said.

Birdie looked at him with a mixture of pity and scorn. 'No!' she said mildly. 'So that's why you've all your stuff in the car!'

Phil blushed. It didn't help that he saw Ruth smile and heard Saskia smother a giggle in the back seat. A fellow, he thought, could really get to hate women if he considered the matter for long enough.

'Go now,' Birdie said. 'I'll see youse in the morning.'

Phil's mind filled with questions, but he doubted he'd get answers if he asked them. They drove off.

'I wish that woman didn't make me feel so inadequate,' Phil said.

Neither Ruth nor Saskia said anything to that, which only made him feel worse. He didn't want to dwell on it, so instead he concentrated on his driving. In a way the drive back to the city seemed unreal to him. They'd done it often before, of course, but now Phil felt peculiar thinking that they were driving their son back to possible danger. But then, even believing in the danger seemed harder the closer they got to the city. Danger? In the middle of a modern housing estate, with its driveways full of cars, its streets full of children on roller blades or playing football, its houses full of microwave ovens and stereos and videos?

When Phil said this to Ruth she nodded. 'I feel the same

way,' she said. 'I'm tempted to think we were rushed into this by two superstitious old country-women.'

'Do you think we were?'

'No. But I don't know why I don't. I wish I did. I do believe there's something very weird going on. What about you?'

Phil said nothing for a long time. 'I never thought I'd see the day,' he said finally, 'when I'd wish I thought my Ma was gone funny in the head. But she's not. Whatever is really going on, she's not. And neither is Birdie.'

'Sunday night,' said Saskia from the back. 'We'll know all after Sunday night.'

'Whoopee,' said Phil sarcastically. He was sure Saskia knew more than she was saying about this business. It was very annoying. Even Ruth seemed in some small way more clued in than he himself felt. It's not a nice feeling to have your nose rubbed in your own ignorance.

In his child-seat Simon sat happily with Tiger Mike, telling his friend about the wonders of the city. They could go to the playground in the park, he told Mike. Mike could go on the swings and the slides with him. There was a big slide that was a little bit scary, but they'd be all right so long as they stuck together. Sticking together was what friends did best.

HOMECOMING

They were close to home when Phil sat up sharply in his seat.

'Janey Mack!' he said.

'What?' Ruth said. 'What is it?'

'Janey Mack!'

'Phil?'

'I'll show you when we get home. I'm sure I'm right.'

'About what?'

'Never mind. I'll show you.'

When they parked in the driveway he went straight into the house without even waiting for the others. Ruth let Simon go in ahead of her, then she and Saskia carried in a couple of the smaller cases. They passed Simon in the hall. He was introducing Tiger Mike to some of the food on the shelves under the stairs.

'That's pasta,' Simon said, pointing to the top shelf. 'It's like straw when it's raw, but it gets like worms when it's cooked.'

Ruth and Saskia dumped the cases in the hall and looked into the living room. Phil was rummaging in the bookshelves. He looked a bit wild.

'What on earth are you looking for?' Ruth asked him.

'That local history book me Ma got me last year. It's around here somewhere.'

He found the book on the bottom shelf and brought it over to the table. He was looking puzzled.

'Tell me,' Ruth said.

Phil tapped the book. 'Birdie Murray didn't always live in our village,' he said. 'I'd half forgotten the story.'

'What story?'

'Back near the start of the century,' Phil said, 'there was an old woman living in our town called ... let me think ... Mrs Crowe. Livvie Crowe. There were weird stories about her still floating around when I was a young fellow. The sort of stories that you heard later about Birdie. Anyway, Mrs Crowe died when she was very old, and left her property to her niece. Nobody had ever known she'd had one, but this girl duly came and took over the property. She was very young, but she was a widow already.'

'And?'

Phil tapped the book again.

'It's in here,' he said. The cover of the book bore the name of his native parish. 'A local history in words and pictures', it said. Phil opened the book and started leafing through the pages.

'What's in there – the story?' Ruth said.

'No, no. The photo.'

'The photo,' Ruth said blankly.

Saskia had never seen her uncle like this. He was actually excited. It made him look quite handsome, she thought. His face looked like there was somebody living in it. Normally you'd think that an emotion would frighten him.

Phil found the photo he was looking for and stopped. 'Look!' he said. 'Look at that!'

The photo took up most of a page. It was a group photograph taken outside a building. 'Committee of the first Co-operative Society, 1911', the caption read. Phil pointed to an old woman in dark clothes.

'But that's Birdie Murray!' Saskia said.

And certainly the figure looked precisely like Birdie Murray, down to the heavy-lidded eyes and slit mouth.

'No it's not,' Phil said. He pointed to the caption. 'It says here it's Mrs Olivia Crowe.'

'But ...'

'Birdie Murray was the niece. She came to town after Livvie Crowe died.'

'So? A family resemblance?' said Ruth.

'Yes. Remember I said that I thought I'd seen Birdie before? She's the spit of her aunt.'

But Ruth wasn't listening. She was staring at the crowd gathered in the background of the photo, villagers watching the mystery of photography in a small Irish village in 1911.

'Phil?' she said. Her whole body felt cold. In the hall she heard Simon introducing Tiger Mike to the noodles. 'Philip?' Her voice shook.

She extended a finger to point at a figure in the background. It was the figure of an old man. He was standing a little apart from the crowd as though they'd left him some room.

Phil looked where she was pointing. He made a noise that wasn't a word, just a strangled sound in his throat.

'But that's not possible,' he said then.

'I know.'

'But there it is.'

'What is it?' asked Saskia. 'Who's that?'

Ruth told her, in a quaking voice. The man she was pointing to was the old man who'd sold them the bed. Obviously it couldn't be the same man, but he looked the very same. Most of the men in the crowd wore waistcoats and collarless shirts, as he did, but this man had the same great height as the bed-vendor. He also had the wire-rimmed glasses, and that unmistakable stain on one cheek.

Phil wanted to think it was a fault in the picture, but the photo was extraordinarily clear for its age.

'I don't like this,' he said.

But there was nothing they could do. Simon had finished introducing Tiger Mike to the various foodstuffs outside, and now had introduced him to the bathroom too. He came in to the living room smiling at them.

'Get the luggage in,' Ruth said to Phil. 'We'll get a Chinese take-away tonight. No way am I going to the supermarket. I won't be able to do anything till all this is over.'

When Phil went to get the bags she turned to Simon. 'And what about you, young man?' she asked. She tried to make herself sound cheerful. 'You didn't sleep in the car. You should have a nap.'

Simon looked at her very seriously.

'No,' he said. 'First Mike has to meet the house. Auntie Birdie said.'

His eyes held hers, and she shivered a little. Her son's eyes were very serious. He knows what he's saying, she thought. I mightn't get it, but he knows exactly what he's talking about. Everyone involved in this does, except me and Phil and Saskia. And I'm not at all sure about Saskia.

She felt Saskia's hand on her wrist and looked at her niece. Saskia was looking at her coolly and evenly. It wasn't a child's look.

'Ruth,' Saskia said, 'I'm certain you can trust Birdie.'

'So am I,' Ruth said. 'So am I. But I'm frightened for Simon.'

Simon, hearing her, took her hand as well. 'It will be all right, Mammy,' he said. 'Birdie says.'

Ruth made herself cheer up. 'Whatever you say, boss,' she said. 'How about some strawberry milk and a video?'

Simon started jumping up and down. 'Cool!' he said.

'I'll get the milk,' Saskia said. She went into the kitchen. Ruth looked at her watch. Four o'clock. She looked around her at the familiar room, at the neatness which said Simon had been away and the first edges of untidiness which said that he was back. She heard her husband putting suitcases down in the hall. He was whistling, a thing that he wasn't much good at. Ruth thought she heard nervousness in the tuneless sound.

She thought of Birdie Murray with her ancient bike. In other circumstances she'd have found the old woman ridiculous or vaguely sinister. Now they were depending on her totally. What if she was just a mad old woman after all, living out her delusions up a lane? What did that make them? She thought of that strange photograph again. The local history book was still lying on the table. Ruth started leafing through it idly. She had a feeling it was going to be a long weekend.

AN EARLY VISITOR

When Phil woke on Sunday he couldn't believe how rested he felt. Ruth was still asleep. Phil could hear the soft sound of Simon's peaceful breathing on the baby intercom. There'd been no screams in the night, no bad dreams.

The digital clock said 8am. Phil heard the change in Simon's breathing that meant he was starting to wake. He got up, grabbed his dressing-gown and went quietly down the stairs. In the kitchen, yawning, he turned on the coffee machine.

Ruth had been oddly distant last night. He'd put it down

to worry, and hadn't said anything. She'd stayed up after he and Saskia went to bed, and he'd already been asleep when she finally came upstairs.

'Do you really think we'll see Birdie tomorrow?' she'd asked him before he went up.

'There's no morning train on Sundays,' he'd pointed out. 'Unless she gets a lift. But nothing that woman does would surprise me.'

Today felt like a normal Sunday morning, the sort they used to have before the dreams came. By the time he got back with the coffee Simon would probably be snuggling in their bed beside his Mammy. Phil filled his son's drinking cup with milk and put it in the microwave. Then he went to the living room, opened the curtains and nearly jumped out of his skin. Birdie Murray was standing outside the window, looking in at him with her blank, unreadable face.

He hurried to the hall and unlocked the door. Birdie was waiting on the step. Her bike was propped up by the wall. Still not fully awake, Phil looked from Birdie to the bike.

'Where did you come from at this hour?' he asked.

'From first Mass,' Birdie said.

Phil's brains felt scrambled. Birdie looked at him with that pitying look she had. 'Are you going to leave me standing on the step?' she asked. 'These mornings are could on ould bones.'

'Yes,' he said. 'No. I mean, I'm sorry. Come in.'

'What about the bike?' Birdie asked. 'I hears terrible stories about thieves in the city.'

Phil looked at the old bike. He couldn't imagine that any light-fingered local youth would find it attractive, unless maybe he had connections with an antique dealer. And Phil suspected that anyone who stole anything of Birdie's would regret it anyway.

'Our local thieves won't be up yet, Mrs Murray,' he said. 'They're probably not long in bed.'

He tried to picture her cycling the eighty-odd miles to the city. It just wasn't possible. Then he thought of what she'd said about Mass. First Mass in the local church hadn't even started yet.

'Where did you go to Mass?' he asked as she came in.

'I went with your Mammy,' Birdie said. 'She sends her regards.'

In the village church? First Mass there would have ended barely a quarter of an hour ago. Phil started to think about that, then gave up. Sometimes it was better just to accept facts. She was here.

Birdie paused by the living room door. 'God bless all here,' she said.

'They're still in bed,' Phil said.

'I know. But God blesses bedrooms as well.'

Yes, Phil thought. Of course you know. Is there anything you don't know, I wonder.

'Plenty,' Birdie said, startling him. 'Didn't I tell you I'd be here this morning?' she said.

'You did, Mrs Murray. But I thought maybe you were joking.'

'Life is too short for joking.'

Phil wondered whether he ought to offer her a cup of tea, but remembered what she'd said to Ruth about never eating and drinking. If that hadn't been a joke, then what had it been? He found Birdie Murray a very hard woman to deal with.

'There was no trouble with the child last night,' Birdie said.

'No,' he said, though it hadn't sounded like a question. 'Nothing. I haven't looked in on him today yet, but he slept peacefully.'

'He's up now,' Birdie said, and indeed Phil heard footsteps upstairs and then Simon's voice, excited, and Ruth's sleepy answers. Mother and child came down the stairs.

'Auntie Bird-ie,' Simon's voice called.

'I'm telling you, son,' Ruth said, 'she's not here.' Then she walked in and saw Birdie standing there. 'Oh!' she said.

'Don't ask,' Phil warned her. 'You'll only get more confused.'

But Ruth looked oddly determined.

'Mrs Murray,' she said, 'I want to ask you something, and I want a straight answer.'

Phil looked at her in surprise. Birdie Murray shrugged. 'Ask me, so,' she said.

The local history book still lay on the table. Ruth picked it up. She opened it at the photo they'd seen yesterday and pointed to the old woman in it.

'Who,' she said, 'is that?'

Birdie Murray didn't even look. 'Livvie Crowe,' she said. 'She was sort of an aunt of mine.'

'Sort of?'

'Aye. Sort of.'

Phil expected Ruth to ask about the old man next, but instead she leafed back through the book to another picture. When he looked at this he felt suddenly very cold.

'First known photograph ever taken of the village,' said the caption.

'And who,' Ruth said, 'is that?'

The picture showed the main street. The road was unpaved, but the buildings had hardly changed. There was only one human figure in the picture, an old woman leading a donkey cart.

The old woman was small and dressed entirely in black.

Her face could be seen clearly. She might have been Birdie Murray, except that she couldn't be; she might have been Livvie Crowe, except that she couldn't be Livvie Crowe either. The date of the picture was given at the end of the caption: 1865.

'That's Kitty Mahon,' Birdie said.

'And who the hell,' Ruth said, exasperated, 'was Kitty Mahon?'

'She was a sort of an aunt of Livvie Crowe's,' Birdie said mildly.

'I see. Tell me, was Livvie Crowe born locally?'

'Born, aye. But she moved away very young, like I did meself. She came back when poor ould Kitty died.'

'Like you came back when Livvie died.'

'Aye. It's odd now you mention it, but that's what happened.'

'And I suppose Kitty Mahon left her property to Livvie Crowe, like Livvie Crowe left it to you.'

'She did, bedad. But what are you asking me?'

Ruth looked cross. 'Mrs Murray,' she said, 'I don't even know what I'm asking you.' She leafed back to the first photograph. Now she pointed to the old man. 'This,' she said. 'Who's this? And if you say you don't know then I'm afraid I won't believe you.'

This time Birdie did look at the picture. 'Ah!' she said softly.

'Well?'

'If I said I didn't know that fella,' Birdie said, 'then I'd be a sort of a liar. Would I be right in thinking he looks a bit like the man that sold youse the bed?'

She asked the question in a voice that brimmed with innocence. It was so different from any tone she'd ever used with either of them that even Phil knew it was false. Ruth simply lost her temper. She spoke with a cold fury.

'Mrs Murray,' she said, 'I'm grateful to you for all that you're doing for us. But I believe in my heart and soul that this man in the picture doesn't just look like the man who sold us the bed. In some way that I don't understand I think that he *is* that man. And I think that in some way you're Livvie Crowe, and probably this Kitty Mahon too.'

Phil looked at her as though she'd gone mad, but Birdie Murray just nodded. She looked from one of them to the other, her thin lips pursed. Then she sighed.

'Look,' she said, gently, 'the first night I came to the child I said I'd tell youse what youse could understand. There's no need for youse to hear more, and no point in it. Do youse believe that I wants to help?'

Ruth didn't hesitate. 'Yes,' she said.

'And do youse believe that I can?'

'Yes.'

'Well then!'

Ruth thought for a little while. 'You're saying,' she said, 'that if you told us straight out all you know, we wouldn't understand it?'

'Aye.'

'Why not? Is it some kind of magic secret?'

Birdie Murray shrugged. 'No more magic nor secret than the sky,' she said, 'or a stone or a tree. But who understands them? Do you?'

'No.'

'Childer understand better nor grown-ups,' Birdie said. She pointed a bony finger at the old man in the photo. 'That's one reason that fellow hates them so much.'

'Does Saskia understand?'

'A bit. She's betwixt and between, do you see. She's not

really grown up. Then again, she've a painter's blood in her. Artists have a better grip on this sort of stuff. Or, better to say, they're happy to let well enough alone, and not try to get a grip on it at all. When you've clothes hanging out on the line you don't grab at the wind that do dry them, you're just content that it's there.'

Her finger was still pointing at the man in the photo. Phil pointed at it too. 'What I'd like to understand better,' he said, 'is the connection between that man and you. There must be one. Who is he?'

Birdie Murray looked at the photograph. 'He have a lot of names,' she said, almost dreamily, 'but he don't keep any of them long. He have only the one true name, and 'twas me gave him that. We were great friends one time. A long time ago.' She sounded almost wistful. 'He went bad,' she said then, her tone hardening. 'So I named him Bad Jack.'

'Did you know he was involved in this?'

'I did. Sure it had to be him. No-one else would be so rude.'

She was, for her, giving very straight answers. Phil tried to think of something else to ask her, but the whole thing was so weird that it was hard even to form questions about it.

'Can you tell us,' Ruth asked, 'just what you're going to do?'

But Birdie shook her head. 'Youse wouldn't understand,' she said. 'Youse wouldn't even hear what I said, just like youse can't see the Pooshipaw. There's no words for the things that I does. Words are only little wriggly things. They're handy in their place, but their place is not here.'

She thought for a bit. Simon was taking all his toys down from the shelves in the corner and bringing them over to introduce them to her.

'Your Ma tells me,' Birdie said to Phil, 'that you're an accountant. Is that right?'

'It is.'

'Did you ever do an audit – ain't that what it's called? You balances a company's books and all that?'

'That's what it's called, yes, an audit. And yes, I've done company audits. But –'

Birdie Murray tapped the photo in the book with a skinny finger. 'Bad Jack's books gets out of order,' she said. Her voice wasn't wistful any more. 'They needs balancing now and again.'

She looked at Phil and grinned coldly, showing him her yellow teeth.

'I does a bit of auditing meself betimes,' she said. 'After me fashion. Think of it like that, if it makes it easier for you: I'm from the auditors.'

Then she turned to Simon, who'd been clamouring for her attention. Within a few minutes she was romping on the floor with him, looking impossibly fit for her age. Ruth went to get dressed. Phil tried to think of more to ask, but he sensed that Birdie's moment of openness was gone. So he made breakfast. When it was ready he and Ruth sat to eat. Simon didn't want to stop playing with Birdie Murray, but she advised him to have his breakfast and he went straight to the table with no argument at all.

'You're sure you'll have nothing, Mrs Murray?' Ruth said.

Birdie Murray made a face. 'No,' she said. 'I'll go and take a look at this famous bed.'

Phil started to tell her where Simon's room was, but she just walked out as he began to speak. Phil made a face. 'I suppose she just knows,' he said sourly.

Ruth shrugged. 'Does that surprise you?'

Her husband sighed. 'No,' he said. 'I suppose not.'

They were still eating when Birdie came back down. They

heard her walk along the hall and open the back door. Phil couldn't control his curiosity. He got up and had a quick look out the back window.

'Well?' Ruth asked.

'She's down the garden looking at the ground,' Phil said. 'God knows what she's at.'

'Ask her when she gets back.'

'I'll ask her nothing! She'd only make me feel like a fool.'

They'd all finished eating by the time Birdie came in.

'Begob,' she said, 'that's a fine big garden out there. Would you not keep a few hens in it?'

'Mrs Murray!' Phil said. 'We're in the middle of the city!'

'Do youse not ate eggs in the city, then?'

Phil said nothing.

'Or a few vegetables would be nice,' Birdie said. 'Sure there's nothing like your own vegetables.'

Phil said nothing again.

Birdie said she wanted to talk to Simon and Tiger Mike; she had a bit of work to do with them, was how she put it.

'What about Saskia?' Phil asked.

'Sure Saskia is asleep,' Birdie said.

'And us?' said Ruth. 'Don't you have any ... instructions for us?'

Birdie Murray thought. 'I can't say as I have,' she said. 'Youse should give the child a good bath before you puts him to bed. That's important.'

'Will it help with ... whatever is going to happen?' Phil asked.

'Yerra, not a bit of it – but it's important to keep childer clean, you know.'

Phil looked very frustrated. 'Yes,' he said sourly. 'So I've read.'

Birdie stared at him. 'God help us all,' she said, 'if you needs to read a book to know that.'

Phil looked as though he was going to scream. Birdie turned to Simon. 'Time to go to work, chap,' she said.

'And Tiger Mike!' Simon said.

'Oh, to be sure,' Birdie said. 'And Tiger Mike.'

Simon swung himself down from the chair and made for the door. Then he looked back at his Mammy and Daddy and smiled at them. 'Simon's not going to go gone!' he said to them, and walked out.

Birdie Murray was closing the door when she thought of something. She looked back in.

'I won't see youse after today,' she said. 'But youse are not to worry. Youse had no need to worry about this from the minute your mammy came to me. Anything new that you find in Simon's room tomorrow, keep it. He'll tell youse.'

Then she went out. Ruth and Phil looked in silence at the closed door. They heard Birdie and Simon climbing the stairs.

'That woman takes great pleasure in getting my goat,' Phil said.

'More fool you,' Ruth said, 'for having a goat that's so easy to get. She's only teasing you.'

'I know that. But it's aggravating.'

'Phil? How did she get here this morning? Surely not on that bike?'

Phil shook his head and sighed. 'I only know what she told me,' he said.

'Which was?'

He sighed again. 'I'll tell you later, but it'll leave you no wiser. I've stopped even wondering about the woman myself. Wondering about her is even more frustrating than talking to her.'

The local history book was still lying open. Phil leafed through it until he reached the group photo of the Co-operative Committee. He studied it.

'That's the old man,' he said. 'That's definitely him.'

'And her. That's Birdie Murray there, whatever name she went by then.'

They both looked at the photo in silence. They were very mixed up, and neither of them liked it. But it would have to do. They knew that really they had no choice. Birdie Murray might be a lot of things they didn't like, but she was on their side. That was the important thing.

'I keep thinking of your mother's story,' Ruth said. 'The one about that man and the dog.'

'Bob Daley?'

'Yes. A good foreman knows better nor to hinder a craftsman while he's working. We'll just have to stay out of the way, Phil. Simon is our son, but this is Birdie Murray's job.'

'I know. I just wish I understood.'

'So do I. But when the telly goes funny and somebody comes to fix it, I don't understand what they're doing either. And I don't expect them to explain the technical bits to me. I don't care so long as the telly works.'

'But at least I believe in electricity. This is ...'

'Magic,' Ruth said.

'Yes. Magic.'

'And we're sitting here with a witch in the house. And an evil creature in our son's bed.'

'No. A creature of evil. Remember?'

'I only wish,' Phil said, 'I could forget.'

A STONE AND A BONE

In the guest bedroom Saskia was having a dream. It was, for her, a very vivid one. She dreamed that she was in the field at Birdie Murray's house. She was sitting by the stream at the bottom of the field, and could just see the roof of the cottage at the top of the slope. There was no sign of Ned or Nora or, for that matter, of Birdie herself. It was a warm day with a blue sky overhead. The place where she sat was by a shallow ford in the quick-running stream. The bed of the stream here was sandy and strewn with rocks and pebbles. Saskia was listening to the ripple of the water on the stones. She could almost imagine that the sound was more than simply musical: she could nearly hear a tune in it.

'And sure why not, if you want?' said a voice from behind her. 'It's your dream, ain't it?'

When Saskia looked she saw Birdie Murray standing behind her.

'Mrs Murray!' she said. 'I'm a bit mixed up. Is this really a dream? Though I can't imagine why else I'd be sitting here in my nightdress.'

Birdie crouched down on her hunkers beside the girl.

'It's a sort of a dream,' she said. 'I wanted to talk to you, but I didn't want to wake you.'

'So I'm not really there.'

'Well you are and you aren't. It depends what you mean by "there".'

'I mean by your stream.'

'Oh you're that, all right. Only you're not all there, if you'll pardon the expression. You're in bed asleep somewhere else as well.'

Saskia looked thoughtful. 'I didn't know that could be done,' she said.

'It can't.'

'But then –'

'Hush, childeen! Don't think about it too much or you'll ruin it. "Can" and "can't" are only two ends of the one stick. Most people lives on the ends of the stick; my sort works in the middle. What we're doing can sort of be done, so I'm sort of doing it. Begob, but people is always full of questions! You're here and I'm here. Let's talk.'

Saskia settled herself more comfortably on the grass. She lifted her nightdress and rested one foot on the bed of the stream, testing the water. It felt pleasantly cool. It hardly covered her toes. She could feel soft sand and hard pebbles under the sole of her foot. The sand and the pebbles felt real.

'All right,' she said to Birdie Murray. 'What will we talk about?'

'About you. About tonight. Are you still willing?'

'Of course. Though I wish ...'

'What?'

'I wish you could tell me more about what I have to do. I do want to get it right.'

Birdie Murray made a face. 'For the first part,' she said, 'you've to do nothing at all – and it's important that you don't do anything. For the second part ...'

She made the face again, then shook her head. 'I just can't tell you exactly,' she said. 'And not because I don't want to. What happens when me and Jack haves it out ... it's not settled. There's very strict rules, and we can't break them, but once we stays inside the rules then we can use any weapons we likes. Except we can't plan beforehand. Else it wouldn't work.'

She shook her head. 'Bedad,' she said, 'that don't even make much sense to me, never mind you. Lord, but I hates words. They're useless when it comes to important things.'

Saskia tried to understand. It was hard, even in a dream. 'My father has this story that he tells,' she said finally, 'about an idea he had for a painting once. He was on a train, and had no drawing stuff with him. So he spent the whole journey planning out the picture, every single detail of it. He even planned the exact shades of colour. He could see in his mind just how it was going to look.'

Birdie Murray looked interested. 'And?' she said.

'Well, he got home and went to his studio. He set up a canvas and took up his palette and brushes. But then, when he stood in front of the canvas, he suddenly realised that he couldn't be bothered actually painting the picture. You see, he'd seen it too clearly in his mind already. He knew how it was going to look; it had no surprises in it for him. And that's why he paints, you see – for the surprises. He lets his instinct guide his hand, he says. He has to make it up right there and then, like the old Japanese masters used to do. I don't know if this is anything like what you're talking about ...'

But Birdie Murray was nodding enthusiastically. 'This is it,' she said. 'This is it entirely. Tonight you'll have to let your instinct guide you. If I could tell you what would happen, what you should do, then I'd be breaking the rules. There'd be no surprises. If you need to do something, you'll know. It must be your doing, not mine. That's important.'

'And there'll be danger? For me, I mean. Real danger?'

'I told you, there have to be a risk. If there's no danger, you can do nothing. Them is the rules.'

'Who made up the rules, Mrs Murray?'

'Yerra, child, who made up the sky? They're just the rules – they're just there. It's the way of these things. So long as you don't join the fight there's no danger. But if you have to do something ...'

'I may get hurt. I know. Would it be a bad hurt, do you know?'

'No, I don't know. And if I did I couldn't tell you.'

Saskia looked at the stream. 'But it could be bad.'

'It could, aye.'

'Could I die?'

'That depends on what you mean by dying.'

Saskia didn't actually know what she meant by dying. It had always seemed a fairly simple thing before. 'Where's Simon?' she asked, to change the subject. She didn't want to frighten herself.

'Simon's in his room,' Birdie said.

'On his own?'

'No, I'm with him.'

Saskia felt like giving some cheeky reply, but realised that Birdie was probably just stating facts. This was all very hard to get your mind around.

'I'll do anything for Simon, Mrs Murray,' she said. 'And I'd be mad to turn down an adventure like this. I'll be there with you tonight, and if I can help then I will. Though I still don't understand why you might need me. Tiger Mike might qualify as "muscle", as you call it, but no-one would call me that.'

Birdie Murray stood up and smoothed down her long skirt. 'There's muscle,' she said, 'and there's muscle. You might say that you could be my element of surprise. Bad Jack is half-expecting me for sure. We're overdue a run-in. But he's definitely not expecting you.'

'And do you always need help?'

'Not always. But I told you, me and Jack's run-in is overdue – way overdue. We all gets old, Saskia. And a bit of help never goes astray. Your feelings for Simon will be help in themselves.'

She pointed down towards the stream. 'Reach in there,' she said, 'and pick out a stone.'

'A stone?'

'Any stone.'

Saskia shrugged and did as she was bid. Without much thought she picked up a bright round pebble and held it up. 'Will this do?' she asked.

'That's grand. Now give it to me.'

Saskia gave her the pebble. Birdie Murray took it and peered at it. She held it up so that the sun glinted off specks of mica buried in it. 'That's granite, that is,' she said. 'That's from the mountains. 'Twould take a couple of thousand years, maybe, for that stone to come down this far and get rounded like that. And when this stone was part of a big rock on a mountaintop, girleen, me and Bad Jack Mackey were ould enemies already.'

She rubbed the stone between her hands, muttering to herself. Then she opened her hands and breathed slowly and evenly on the pebble. When she handed it back to Saskia the stone was still warm from the rubbing. Birdie reached into a pocket lost in the folds of her skirt. She took something from the pocket and held this out too to Saskia. When Saskia took it, she found herself holding what looked like a little bone. The bone was small and straight and dark with age.

'You get plenty of rest today,' Birdie Murray said. 'Go to

bed early. Remember, you're on the night shift tonight. When you goes asleep put that stone in your right hand and that bone in your left. Keep them in your hands all the time that you're with me. All the time – understood?'

Saskia was looking at the bone. She couldn't recognise what it might be from. 'What sort of bone is this?' she asked.

''Tis part of a finger,' Birdie Murray said.

Saskia nearly dropped the dark, stick-like thing. 'A human finger?' she asked.

'Aye. Sure there's not much else round these parts with fingers, is there?'

'Is it ...' Saskia wasn't sure what she wanted to ask, never mind how to ask it. 'Is it anyone I know?' she said at last, feeling foolish at the sound of her own words.

'Sort of,' Birdie said. 'It's sort of mine, in a roundabout class of a way.'

'Yours!' said Saskia. When she looked up she saw that Birdie was grinning.

'You might say it belonged to one of my predecessors,' Birdie said. She chuckled. The sound was like a cousin of the music of the water on the stones.

Saskia held the bone very gingerly. 'Mrs Murray,' she said, 'if this is a prop to impress me, like that stuff for Ruth and Phil, then you don't really have to ...'

But then she noticed that Birdie Murray wasn't there any more, though the chuckle seemed almost to hang in the air after her. Saskia blinked with surprise. When she opened her eyes she was lying in bed in Phil and Ruth's guest bedroom. She felt things in her hands. When she held the hands up and opened them she saw that she was holding a pebble and a bone. The stone was warm, as though someone had been rubbing it.

'Ma-mmy! Da-ddy!' Simon's voice called from his room. 'Birdie's going gone!'

In the kitchen Ruth and Phil looked at each other. They'd heard nobody coming downstairs. But sure enough, when they went up they found Simon standing behind the closed stairgate. He was on his own except for Tiger Mike. There was no sign anywhere of Birdie Murray. Phil went into his and Ruth's bedroom and opened the window. He leaned his head out and looked down. Birdie's bike was gone too.

'She does it on purpose!' Ruth heard him muttering. 'The damned woman does it on purpose!'

Saskia came yawning from her room. 'I had the strangest dream,' she said. 'I thought Birdie Murray was here.'

Phil made a sour face. 'You know, that's funny,' he said. 'So did I.'

'But it seemed so real,' Saskia said. 'I could hear her voice. When I woke up properly I had to persuade myself that it wasn't possible.'

'No,' Phil said, in a voice like vinegar. 'It wasn't, was it?'

Saskia gathered that this wasn't the best moment to talk about Birdie Murray. She was suddenly very hungry. She went downstairs thinking of bones and stones and breakfasts.

BACK TO WORK

It wouldn't be exactly true to say the Pooshipaw woke up, because Pooshipaws don't sleep like us. They don't do anything like us, really, but in particular they don't sleep and wake.

In many ways Pooshipaws are hard things to talk about. By our standards they're not really there at all, at least not in any way that we understand. Sometimes they're sort of there, and that's their version of being awake; when they're not sort of there then they're sort of somewhere else, and that's their version of being asleep.

The Pooshipaw had been sort of somewhere else all the time the family was on holiday. The somewhere else was a very pleasant place, or at least it was pleasant if you were a Pooshipaw.

It was a place like an endless rubbish dump, a great, almost grassless field covered with mounds of stinking dirt and rusting machines. The air there was rich with the smells of rot, which to unreformed Pooshipaws is a sweeter scent than any other.

The sky above the place was dull grey and filled with dark, smoky clouds. It was such a very dirty place that even these clouds smelled of rot.

Now in that stinking place the Pooshipaw did something a bit like waking up. He scratched his fur and looked around, sniffing. He'd woken feeling grumpy and unrested. If he didn't know better, he'd think that he'd had a bad dream. But that was impossible. Pooshipaws don't have dreams, good or bad. The Master had told him that, and the Master was always right. In some ways Pooshipaws are a little bit like machines, the Master said: they're either turned on or turned off.

Right now the Pooshipaw was puzzled and displeased. Just for a moment on waking he'd seemed to smell something in the air that he'd never smelled here before, that he'd never imagined he would smell here. He found the smell very unpleasant. It was the faint smell of flowers.

The scent was so faint that the Pooshipaw wasn't even sure that he really smelled it. But then he got the other smells, the ones that he'd been waiting for: the twin smells of Simon being back and of its being night-time in that other place we think of as our world.

The Pooshipaw forgot the smell of flowers. He started to hum to himself almost happily. The Pooshipaw's humming was no better than his singing.

The Pooshipaw went to his favourite rubbish pile and picked some ripe bones. He shook the flies off and stuck the bones in his pocket. There was a lot he disliked about humans, but one of the things he disliked most about them was the disgusting food they ate. He'd never managed to find a well-matured bone in their world, although he'd scrounged through many rubbish bins and tips there in his time.

'Time to go to work,' he said to no-one in particular, in that place that was no place in particular. Then he was standing in Simon's room. He held his breath against the sweet, clean smell of the place. It always took him a little while to adjust, and he was sure that he'd never get used to it. He didn't like spending any more time in this place than he had to.

Simon slept peacefully in the racing-car bed. The Pooshipaw looked at him with a mixture of contempt and something almost like fondness.

'Poor ould simple Simon,' he said.

In a way you couldn't help but pity humans. They were so puny. The Pooshipaw felt guilty when he pitied them, but he really couldn't help himself. It was a weak spot. He could never understand how they'd managed to take over this world in the first place. Even here there were other animals much worthier. The maggot, now, was an attractive beast, as indeed was the rat.

Mind you, the Pooshipaw had to admit that the humans were gradually improving the place. He liked to think of himself as fair. He'd give credit where credit was due. Humans did show some talent for making dirt. They were gradually turning this world into a more pleasant place for those like himself, not to mention the maggots and rats.

But it was no time for philosophy. 'Worky, worky,' the Pooshipaw said to himself.

It was a pity the child had gone away. It would have weakened the work he'd done already. The first thing to do was to check just how much of his influence was left.

The Pooshipaw half-closed his sulphur-coloured eyes. The smoky light inside them came on. He bent over Simon and looked inside him. What he saw there shocked him.

'Snot on a skate!' the Pooshipaw said.

There was no hollowness at all. The boy might never have had a single visit from a Pooshipaw. There wasn't a trace of all that hard work. If anything he was more whole than when the Pooshipaw had looked first, all those weeks ago now. The Pooshipaw had never heard of such a thing.

'It's not supposed to work like this,' he said. He scratched his head, baffled. 'Tch! Tch! Tch!' he said, clicking his thick tongue.

He looked around the room. Nothing new, except a ratty-looking old toy. A smiling tiger. The tiger looked back at him with blank and lifeless eyes.

'Grrrr,' said the Pooshipaw to the tiger. The tiger said nothing, just kept smiling.

Simon mumbled something in his sleep. He was smiling too. The Pooshipaw glowered at him.

'Wretched little pup!' he said. 'Dream sweet while you can! You're in for the advanced nightmare course, little sausagey man!'

Whatever had happened, of course, it wasn't the boy's fault; but the Pooshipaw's fairness didn't run very deep.

'I'll mortify you!' he muttered to the unsuspecting child. 'I'll scarify you! It'll be gibbering you'll be, and not screaming! And as for them big ones ...'

He glowered in the direction of Phil and Ruth's room. Not that it could be their fault either. They were just two more hairless monkeys. In fact the Pooshipaw couldn't think of any reason for Simon's restoration. It had to be some freak accident. A Pooshipaw's work was always damaged when a child went away. This was just an extreme case.

For a moment the Pooshipaw thought of his Master. He wouldn't be pleased. The Pooshipaw flinched when he thought of the punishment the Master might give him. He was an expert at punishment, the Master. He seemed to enjoy it.

The Pooshipaw made himself stop thinking of the Master. It wasn't nice. So the child was whole again: very well, the Pooshipaw would just have to work harder at making him hollow. And if he worked well, maybe the Master wouldn't punish him so much this time.

Pooshipaws don't really think much. They do learn from experience, and get more sly with age – and they live for a very long time, in so far as they're alive at all. But they're not made for thinking, only for doing their masters' dirty work. And as is the way with these things, even among humans, the masters of those who do dirty work rarely tell the doers of that work all they know.

This Pooshipaw was not, by the standards of Pooshipaws, very old. His Master hadn't warned him that there were other forces at work in the world, forces not at all friendly to Pooshipaws. So the Pooshipaw went to work now with no sense of danger. He crossed his lamplike eyes and began to imagine the green car. When all was said and done, it was good to be back at work. It was what he lived for. The Pooshipaw dribbled with anticipation.

'Someone is in for a bad night tonight,' he said with some relish.

He was perfectly right. In a way.

IN THE GREEN CAR

This time there was no conversation before the bad dream started. When Simon woke up they were already in the green car, and he was already dreaming.

It hadn't taken Simon long to figure out that he wasn't really steering the green car. He'd realised that much by the third or fourth dream. He'd been so frightened by then that his hands shook. They'd slipped from the steering wheel, but the car had kept driving and turning corners without crashing.

Simon had realised then that the green car was like one of the rides in the supermarket, which were machines shaped like cars or fire-engines. You sat in them, put money in, pressed a button, and they started to move and make driving noises. There was a steering wheel that you could turn, but the machine went on whether you turned the wheel or not. It was only a game of pretend.

The green car was far scarier than the toy car rides, but it worked in that same way. Simon decided at the time not to let the Pooshipaw see that he'd found this out. The Pooshipaw seemed amused by Simon's fear of driving. He laughed at it. Some instinct told Simon that it might be useful to let the Pooshipaw keep thinking that he was more stupid than he really was.

In any case there was more than enough to be afraid of on the night-time drives. Anything that helped at all was welcome.

Simon had never again since the first night seen the sign that said START HERE – GOODBYE! Each night afterwards the drive had started somewhere down the road, and every night it had started further on. So he was surprised now to find they were once again driving under the big sign.

'Did you see that?' the Pooshipaw demanded. 'Did you see that sign?'

'I saw,' Simon said.

'You're the first child that ever saw that twice,' said the Pooshipaw. 'All my work with you was wasted! Down the lavatory, every bit of it!'

'But the Pooshipaw likes to take his time,' Simon said. 'You said.'

The Pooshipaw made an ugly sound. 'Taking your time is

one thing,' he said primly. 'Wasting it is another thing entirely.'

It was the first time he'd been with the Pooshipaw that Simon wasn't even slightly afraid. Birdie had told him that everything would be all right, and his faith in her was absolute. When he looked at her he didn't see the person that his parents saw. The person that he did see was surrounded by the same warm, loving glow that his Nanny had.

Simon had confessed to Birdie that he felt some pity for the Pooshipaw. It was easier to talk about things with Birdie because they didn't just use words when they talked. Birdie understood everything that Simon felt about everything, even the mixed-up bits.

And now that he wasn't afraid of the Pooshipaw he had time to study him a bit more. The smell of dirt from the creature was awful, but underneath it was hidden another smell hardly less strong – a smell of loneliness.

Grown-ups couldn't smell loneliness, Birdie had told him. There were lots of important things they couldn't do. They couldn't smell niceness, or see goodness. They couldn't see the lights around people, or read what they meant.

It was all very hard to believe, though since Birdie said it then it must be true. And it did explain a lot about their behaviour. Simon couldn't imagine how they got by at all. Grown-ups were to be pitied nearly as much as the Pooshipaw. He never wanted to lose this sight, to be blind to the glow around Nanny or the fierce silver light he could see around Saskia sometimes.

Birdie had told Simon how to make friends with a Pooshipaw, though it was too early to try it with this one.

'It's like making rabbit stew,' Birdie said. 'First you haves to catch your rabbit.' And then she'd stopped herself and apologised, because Simon was very fond of rabbits and didn't like the notion of a rabbit stew.

Pooshipaws wove dreams, Birdie had said. There were no better storytellers alive. If you made friends with one, you'd never need a television. The idea of not needing a television, and so never seeing Sesame Street again, didn't make a lot of sense to Simon.

'But sure if you were friends with a Pooshipaw,' Birdie said, 'you'd have Sesame Street in your bedroom every night while you were asleep. Man alive! Wouldn't that be better nor ould pictures on a bit of glass? Sure you could live half your life in Sesame Street!'

Simon found this idea rather attractive. In the green car now he sneaked a look over at the Pooshipaw, who was sucking a bone and muttering darkly to himself. His big yellow eyes were squeezed half-shut, and he had a very sour look on his furry face. The notion of having a creature like this for a friend still seemed unlikely.

They were coming to the place where Simon had seen the crashed car on the night of that first drive. Simon felt a shiver running through him. He hoped he wouldn't see the two broken figures lying by the road. He'd only glimpsed the Mammy figure and the Daddy figure as the green car sped by, but the picture had stayed with him ever since. He remembered the way they'd looked, with Daddy's legs at strange angles and Mammy's long hair stained with blood. It wasn't real, of course: his real Mammy and Daddy had been safe asleep in bed at the time. But it hadn't been nice at all.

Ahead of them now Simon saw a black-bordered road sign. ACCIDENT BLACK SPOT said the words he couldn't read. But he recognised the sign. Desperately he pictured Birdie Murray in his mind.

The Pooshipaw seemed to cheer up when he saw the sign ahead. 'Eh, Sausage,' he said. 'Just look where we are! You'd better drive careful. We don't want to crash the green car, now, do we?' And he wheezed a laugh and fluttered the fingers of his two left hands in a mockery of fear.

They came to the corner beyond which the crashed car had been. But now as they turned they saw the same car, upright, parked neatly in a lay-by that hadn't been there last time. There was a tablecloth spread on the grass, and on the tablecloth were the makings of a picnic. Beside the cloth sat a man and a woman. The man was Daddy, the woman was Mammy. Daddy's arm was draped around Mammy's shoulders. As the green car passed them they looked up, smiled, and waved.

The Pooshipaw made an awful choking sound. 'Bile on a bike!' he said. 'That can't be!'

He swivelled around in his seat to look back as they turned the corner. When he looked back he saw something in the back seat that made him make even stranger sounds. Simon smelled nice smells he knew – the dry, starchy smell of Birdie and the silvery, relation smell of Saskia. There was another smell too, a warm, ripe, furry, pussycat sort of smell. It was mixed up with a faraway scent of the seaside on a hot day. He'd never smelled the furry seaside smell before, but he liked it straight away.

'You drive careful, now,' said the voice of Birdie Murray from the back. 'I gets nervous in a car.'

The Pooshipaw made more peculiar sounds. He sounded like he was choking on something.

'Shove up there, Mike, yeh brute,' said the voice of Birdie Murray. 'This poor child beside me have no room at all. And while you're at it, get to work.'

Simon was dying to turn around. The Pooshipaw was staring into the back seat with a look of complete shock on his face.

A great striped paw came down and rested on Simon's shoulder. He felt its weight, and the rippling of strong muscles under the black and orange fur.

A similar paw came down on the back of the Pooshipaw's seat. White, tufted toes dangled just in front of the Pooshipaw's snout. Long, curved claws slid out and pricked at the Pooshipaw's fur. The Pooshipaw sat with his mouth hanging open. Simon could smell his rank breath.

A striped head even bigger than the Pooshipaw's leaned down between the two front seats. It swivelled until two huge yellow eyes were looking at Simon with a friendly, dreamy gaze. The eyes looked awfully like Birdie's. Beneath the eyes a huge mouth opened. Sharp white teeth showed in a friendly grin. The warm, furry smell was overpowering.

'Tiger Mike!' said Simon. Birdie had told him that Mike would help, but he hadn't expected anything like this. He was astonished.

One of the big yellow eyes winked very slowly. 'Hi, man,' Tiger Mike said. 'I, like, dig your wheels.'

His wheels? Simon guessed Mike meant the green car. He was about to explain that the car wasn't his when Mike sensed some movement in the Pooshipaw. The big tawny head swivelled instantly, and the tiger's lemon eyes bored into the Pooshipaw's sulphur-coloured ones.

'Go ahead, punk,' Tiger Mike said to the Pooshipaw. 'Make my day.'

In the Pooshipaw's eyes Simon saw something that he'd never expected to see there: sheer raw fear.

HIJACKERS

In the back seat of the green car Saskia wondered whether this was what it felt like to have your mind boggle. It seemed only moments before that she'd lain in bed and hoped for sleep. Maybe it really *was* only moments before. But she wasn't in bed now – at least she didn't feel like she was, although Birdie had warned that for her this part could be no more than a dream. Saskia hoped that other people's dreams weren't all like this; if they were then she was missing out on even more than she'd suspected. But the bone and the stone in her hands reminded her that this dream was different: it was only a sort of dream, as Birdie might say.

'Your Nanny wanted to come,' Birdie said to Simon. 'But there was no room. She was afraid you'd be afraid.'

'Simon's not afraid with Mike and Birdie and Saskia,' Simon said.

'Of course you're not afraid, Simon,' Birdie said. 'Ain't that what I said to your Nanny? "He'll have no fear with us there, May," says I. "And I have to bring the painter's daughter with me. And sure what would you be wanting, at your age, on a wild ride like that in the middle of the night?" But she missed the Old Folks' Mystery Tour this year, do you see, and it took me a good long while to persuade her to stay home.'

Birdie's voice was chatty as she spoke. It was as though she'd forgotten about the Pooshipaw. But the Pooshipaw hadn't forgotten about her. From the back seat Saskia saw him sitting there, a dumpy green heap in a hat. He was frozen with shock, still staring back with bulging eyes at Mike and Birdie. His face showed a terrible mixture of surprise and fear. Tiger Mike was tickling the fur of the Pooshipaw's chin with one white claw. The claw looked as long as a knitting-needle.

'Coochie coo, man,' Tiger Mike said in a low, growling purr to the Pooshipaw.

'I..rr..ngg..oo..fnrf,' said the Pooshipaw.

'There's no need,' Birdie said, 'for that class of language. Not in front of the childer. Now. We have business to do. Stop the car.' When she spoke to the Pooshipaw, Birdie's voice wasn't chatty at all. It was as cold as ice.

'I don't know how to stop,' Simon said, starting to worry.

'That's fine, love,' Birdie said. 'Sure you know, don't you, that you're not really driving?'

Her voice changed again when she talked to Simon. It grew warm and cuddly. When she next spoke it was to the Pooshipaw again, and the frost was back.

'Stop this yoke now,' she said.

The Pooshipaw seemed to be recovering a bit. His eyes were fixed on the long claw tickling his chin, and his voice shook a bit when he spoke, but his words were defiant enough.

'I don't know what you are, woman,' he said, 'but you've no business here. Nobody bosses me around in my own nightmare!'

'No?' Birdie said.

'No! And as for this animal you have with you, you needn't think I'm afraid of him. Bully-boy tactics don't impress me, I'll have you know. I'll make a tiger-skin rug out of him.'

There was a sound then that Simon had never expected to hear in these dreams: the sound of warm laughter. Oh, the

Pooshipaw had laughed a few times when they were in the green car, right enough, but it had been a dirty, nasty laugh, with slime in it.

The laugh Simon heard now wasn't like that. It was a happy, girlish sound, a clear laugh with music in it. It was a sound that made you happy, that made you want to laugh along with it.

The Pooshipaw didn't like the laugh at all. He flinched when he heard it. Its very happiness seemed to hurt him almost physically.

The laugh was coming from Birdie Murray. It didn't stop. After a while the Pooshipaw started to cower a bit. His great head sank down into his shoulders. He put his filthy paws up to cover his ears, but Tiger Mike pricked the long claw into his green fur. The Pooshipaw's head shot up. His paws stayed frozen in mid-air. Birdie kept laughing. The Pooshipaw looked like he was going to get sick.

Simon started to laugh along with Birdie. He couldn't help it. Her laugh seemed to creep up on him and tickle him. Saskia, feeling the same tickle, joined in. Even Tiger Mike chuckled.

In Saskia's case, the laughter was partly from shock. She was looking at the passing scenery and feeling the warm leather upholstery of the car. She was staring almost fondly at the matted green fur of the Pooshipaw, and with something like awe at the huge presence that was now Tiger Mike.

Fear was the last thing on her mind. Was this really a dream? Did people see stuff like this every night? Seeing Birdie Murray's stream was one thing; this was another thing entirely. Although she laughed, she could as easily have cried. She'd been missing so much! 'This is really something else,' she muttered to no-one in particular.

Birdie Murray stopped laughing and turned to her. 'Sure everything,' she said, 'is something else, child. That's the way of the world.' Then she started that great laugh again, as though she hadn't stopped at all, and in a moment Saskia was once again laughing along.

'Stop doing that!' the Pooshipaw shouted at the laughers.

Birdie didn't stop. The Pooshipaw groaned. Simon actually pitied him. Maybe if the Pooshipaw asked nicely ...

'What's the magic word?' he asked the unfortunate creature, trying to give him a hint.

'PLEASE!' screamed the Pooshipaw. 'Please stop!'

Birdie stopped laughing abruptly. 'Stop the car,' she said coldly. 'And no tricks.'

The green car slowed down and drew in carefully by the side of the road. Saskia controlled herself. This was no time for self-pity. The Pooshipaw, she saw, was actually shivering. He was looking at Birdie with blank terror. He seemed far more afraid of her than of Tiger Mike.

The Pooshipaw whimpered and shook. 'You poor brute,' Birdie said. Her voice was not unkind now. 'You don't know who I am, do you?'

'You're ... you're a hijacker!' the Pooshipaw said. He was nearly crying. 'An interfering ould biddy getting in the way of a Pooshipaw that's trying to do an honest night's work.'

'Honest? Aye, sure I suppose you're honest enough by your lights.'

'I'm supposed to be the boss here!' the Pooshipaw said.

'Here and only here,' Birdie said. 'But the real boss is Bad Jack Mackey.'

The Pooshipaw looked even more frightened, if that was possible. 'You know the Bad Man?' he asked in a voice hardly more than a whisper. 'You know his Name?'

'I gave him the name,' Birdie said. 'Sure didn't I mind him one life and he only a babby? Aye, and if I'd knew the way he'd turn out I wouldn't have been so careful with the minding. I saved that cur's life one time. One time too many.' There was something very frightening about the way she said the last four words.

The Pooshipaw's eyes grew bigger as he looked at the old woman in the back. Tiger Mike looked at Simon and winked again.

'What are you?' the Pooshipaw asked Birdie.

'In the heel of the hunt,' Birdie Murray said, 'I'm your destiny. One way or another. Get out of the car.'

The Pooshipaw hesitated, but Mike turned to him again and purred. Saskia had never imagined that a purr could sound so dangerous.

Tiger Mike and the Pooshipaw got out by the side of the road. Saskia got out too and stood looking up at Tiger Mike.

Now that Simon could see Tiger Mike properly he hardly believed his eyes. He had no doubt that this great beast really was his old friend, but the change in him was very impressive. Mike was enormous here, a great, lithe animal, glowing with power and health. His fur seemed almost to shine. He towered above the dumpy, smelly figure of the Pooshipaw. Simon couldn't figure out how Mike had fitted into the green car.

From the way Saskia was looking at Mike, she obviously felt the same as Simon. This was the first real sight of Saskia that Simon had had too. She was wearing her nightdress, and was surrounded by her silvery glow. Her whole body was ghostly and almost transparent. It didn't seem to bother her, though. Her face was shining with excitement, and her eyes were big and wide. As he looked she turned and met his eyes. She grinned and made a face at him.

'This is big-time dreaming, kiddo!' she said, almost hopping from foot to foot with excitement. Though her words were clear her voice sounded faint and had an odd sort of echo off it. It sounded like it was coming from somewhere far away.

'Young Saskia wanted to come along,' Birdie told him. 'But she's not really here – even less than we are. She have no part in this job of work. She's only here to look now. Her time will come in a while. Youse can talk about it another time.'

She got out of the car, opened Simon's door, and picked him up in her arms. Looking at her, Saskia noticed that Birdie too was different. The change was far less dramatic than the change in Mike, but it was just as definite. Birdie looked younger and taller. There was more black in her hair. Her face was rounder and softer, and glowed with something like excitement.

Birdie saw the thought in Saskia's mind. 'I'm always like this when me blood is up,' she said. 'I loves a good fight. I lives for me work.'

The Pooshipaw looked over at her. 'Me too,' he said glumly. 'I used to, anyhow.'

Birdie looked at him. 'Oh, aye,' she said. 'Sure I knows that. We·have a few things in common, yourself and meself.'

Tiger Mike looked at her. 'Man, what a weird thing to say,' he said.

Birdie smiled at him. 'You're a good beast, Mike,' she said. 'But you're a simple soul.'

The Pooshipaw was a sad creature when you saw him standing beside Tiger Mike. He seemed to have sunk in on himself. No-one could be afraid of him now. He looked beaten and sad, just a lost, dirty creature by the roadside. Birdie's laugh had done it, Saskia knew; it had hurt the

Pooshipaw in some deep way she didn't understand. The fight between Birdie and the Pooshipaw was a funny sort of fight, but for all of its oddity Saskia knew it was a genuine battle. But she had no doubt at all that the battle was over now, and that Birdie Murray had won it.

Part of Simon felt he should be happy to see the Pooshipaw look so beaten, but somehow the happiness wouldn't come. Instead he just felt sad for the miserable beast, sad to see any creature looking so forlorn.

'Well, Simon,' Birdie said. 'There's your monster now. He was going to hurt you, you know. Hurt you bad. Do you want me to hurt him instead?'

It was the last thing Simon wanted. He shook his head.

'Don't hurt the Pooshipaw,' he said. 'The Pooshipaw is very sad now.' He looked fiercely into Birdie's eyes. Birdie smiled at his determined face.

'Begob, son,' she said, 'but ould Jack Mackey picked himself a tough little chicken to pluck this time round.'

'You can hurt Bad Jack,' Simon offered.

Birdie Murray smiled. She gave a chuckle that was downright nasty. '*Leanaveen,*' she said. 'You leave ould Jackie to Birdie. I told you one time that we ates Pooshipaws for our breakfast. But Bad Jack, now, he's more of a slap-up dinner. And we does get hungry, you know, for a nice slap-up dinner betimes.'

Her voice when she said this had a crooning, dreamy sound that was somehow scarier than anything else she'd said. Her smile was still bright as she turned once again to the Pooshipaw. By now he was looking at her with a look so defeated that it didn't even hold any fear. This old woman had crumbled his universe with her nuclear laugh.

'And now, mister man,' Birdie said to the Pooshipaw, 'what are we going to do about you?'

THE FOX AND THE HEDGEHOG

The surprise of having outsiders turn up at all had unnerved the Pooshipaw. Nothing he knew had prepared him for such an event. The surprise had been total, and in itself nearly enough to take the fight out of him. The big tiger and the grinning human child were bad enough, but he'd sensed immediately that, if it came to a fight, then it was the old woman who would be the greatest danger.

Birdie was taking no chances: the Pooshipaw would lose any fight there might be, but she didn't want him to fight at all. If he did, she would have to destroy him. The rules of the game left no other way for dealing with monsters. So she'd done the thing that Simon had heard as laughter, a terrible, witchy laughter that was as sharp a weapon as a sword when it was used against you.

The sound of that laughter had been an awful torment to the Pooshipaw, and the way she talked about the Master had been the last straw. She had known the Name; she said she'd given that name to the Bad Man, and somehow the Pooshipaw knew she wasn't lying. He could sense the power in her. He'd never known that such power could lie in a human, if she was a human. The Pooshipaw couldn't really tell, and this in itself frightened him badly.

He stood by the road now, his fur lank, his face bleak. The smell of his fear covered even the smell of his dirt.

'What are you going to do with me?' he asked.

'Well,' Birdie said, 'that's up to you.'

The Pooshipaw looked surprised.

'You were made the way you are,' Birdie said. Her voice wasn't entirely unkind. The Pooshipaw wondered why she wasn't just scorching him out of existence. He had no doubt that she could. Was she like the Master – did she like giving pain slowly?

'You're a dirty, foul thing that loves foulness and dirt,' Birdie said, but still the Pooshipaw didn't hear any blame in her voice. 'A destroyer of innocent childer,' Birdie said. 'You were made bad by a bad man, Bad Jack Mackey. And where's ould Jack tonight, I wonder, while you're out doing his dirty work for him? Do you know?'

'No,' the Pooshipaw said.

'Well, I'll tell you where he is. He's off laughing at you. Do you think he have any respect for you?'

The buried memories of a thousand hurts and insults stirred in the Pooshipaw's mind.

Birdie put Simon sitting on the bonnet of the green car. It was the first time he'd seen it from the outside. It was a lovely old car, an antique. He wished he had a toy like that.

She took a step towards the Pooshipaw. The Pooshipaw flinched. He could feel the depths of the old woman's power now, could almost see it rippling the dream-air around her as she got closer. The tiger was strong, but it was strong with the same kind of strength as his own. He could fight it, even if he lost the fight.

The old woman's power was different. The Pooshipaw had felt it in that laugh: that had stung him more than anything he'd ever felt. When she laughed he'd seen himself through her eyes, and the sight had lashed him like a whip. Worse still was the urge that had come with it, the urge to look at himself again through those old eyes and join in laughing at the comic sight he saw.

Birdie saw his thoughts. 'You never done a good thing in your life,' she said. 'Because you were made so you wouldn't be able to do a good thing. That's the meaning of the two left hands, d'you see: that you're one-sided. Two right ones would be the same. You were made so the smallest thing you done would be hurtful to someone. It's not your own badness, you know. Not a bit of it is.'

She spoke with complete confidence. A small seed was touched in the Pooshipaw's black heart. Suddenly he found himself looking to this weird old creature for a new thing in his life: a crumb of comfort.

'You done terrible things,' Birdie said. She sounded almost sorry for him. 'Unspeakable things. And you'll always be a contrary beast – there's no helping that. But Bad Jack Mackey made you to do his dirty work and take the blame on yourself, so that he'd have none. He made you to take his guilt. Do you know that? Did you ever think about it?'

The Pooshipaw looked at her for a long time. When he finally answered, his voice had a kind of dignity to it. 'I can't afford,' he said, 'to think about it.'

Saskia could hear the black misery behind the words. She felt a wave of pity for the ugly heap of fur. She longed to say something comforting to the Pooshipaw, but that might be interfering. Besides, what would she say? She sensed from the broken creature a huge and horrible misery and a loneliness such as she couldn't even imagine. What useful words of comfort could a happy girl come up with in the face of such despair?

'Things don't have to be like this,' Birdie said. 'I can change you.'

The Pooshipaw studied her very carefully now. Was this old woman really stronger than the Bad Man? He thought of the vengeance the Master might take.

'Bad Jack Mackey,' Birdie said, 'will do nothing to anyone for a long time. He made you to take his blame. But it don't work like that in the end. Bad Jack is going to be put out of business. The auditors are in.'

The Pooshipaw licked his fat lips with his rough tongue. Badness was all he knew. It was the only pleasure he was able to have. Nice things made him throw up.

'I don't understand what you're offering,' he said.

'You can't understand. The understanding ain't in you. Ould Jack made sure of that. But you can trust, I think. He had to make you able to trust, otherwise you wouldn't be able to trust him.'

The Pooshipaw stood on one foot. Then he stood on the other. Then he stood on the first foot again.

'What do I say?' he asked.

'You say Yes or you say No.'

'And if I say No? You'll destroy me, won't you?' He didn't doubt that she could. Very easily, too. He knew that now.

'I will,' Birdie said. 'I'll have to. But I don't think you'd really mind that.'

The Pooshipaw looked up in the air at nothing in particular. He was very confused.

'The fox knows many tricks,' he said. 'But the hedgehog knows the one big trick. Did you ever hear that saying?'

'I did.'

'You're like the fox,' the Pooshipaw said. 'No offence meant.'

'None taken. Sure foxes are grand creatures, so long as they stays out of the henhouse.'

'Meself,' said the Pooshipaw, 'I'm like the hedgehog. You're asking me to give up my one big trick, and to trust I'll learn more. But it's hard to give up what you know when it's the only one thing. I can't know what I'd gain, but I do know what I'd lose.'

Birdie Murray sighed. She poked a bony finger in the dream air. The finger went right through the air and exposed a dark, ragged hole. A sick smell of rot leaked from the hole.

'Look,' she said. 'There's your world, like an ould painted rag over a cesspit. As black as the hob of hell, and twice as empty. I offers you colours. I offers you growing. I offers you the real world. All of it – the good and the bad.'

The Pooshipaw was looking at her very carefully now.

'I offers you,' Birdie Murray said, 'more!'

'More?'

'More!'

Still the Pooshipaw hesitated. You could see that he was very mixed up.

'I can fix that ould hand for you if you like,' Birdie Murray said. 'Give you a right and a left, like a natural creature. We all have two sides, you know, if we're natural!'

The Pooshipaw looked down at his two left hands. For all the muscles in his arms, the hands hung limp like two green dead birds. They were exactly alike, and yet they looked mismatched: some things simply shouldn't be the same.

'And friends, of course,' Birdie said. 'You'd have friends.'

She sounded as though she were offering him some incredible treasure. The Pooshipaw looked at her with something very like hunger.

'Friends?' he said. He seemed to have trouble saying the word.

Saskia yearned to speak out, to call to the creature that he could come home with her and shout at the wild winds in winter. She thought he might like that, somehow. She was just about to say something when Birdie Murray turned and stared at her. It was the same stare she'd given Phil in the kitchen on that first night, and even here in a dream it had the same effect on Saskia. She stood paralysed, her mouth half-open, words that would never be spoken half-formed on her tongue. Then Saskia controlled herself, and closed her mouth, and Birdie Murray looked away.

'Simon?' Birdie said. Simon looked at the Pooshipaw. The creature looked frightened and broken and more lonely than anything he'd ever seen.

'I'll be your friend,' Simon said loudly, decisively, truly.

'And you and Mike,' Birdie said, 'will be inseparable. You'll have to get used to him, mind – but then he'll have to get used to you, too.'

The Pooshipaw looked at Tiger Mike, and Tiger Mike looked at the Pooshipaw. Mike looked doubtful, then he smiled.

'Sure,' he said. 'Sure. Why not?'

The Pooshipaw shuddered. Then with a visible effort he pulled himself up and stood straight. He looked from one of them to the other. Saskia, forbidden to interfere, felt her hands clenched into fists with tension as she watched. She licked her dry dream lips and willed the Pooshipaw to speak. The furry green creature drew itself up to its full height, such as it was. It opened its mouth to speak the one word it must say.

BETWIXT AND BETWEEN

Saskia stood in the dark garden and licked her dry lips. She clutched the pebble tight in her right hand and the bone in her left. They felt hard and real, yet when she looked down she could see right through the hands that held them.

A small breeze whispered through the garden's trees, sounding sinister to Saskia's nervous ears. In front of her the old house was a black mass in the darkness. A dim light showed through the drawn curtains of a ground-floor window. Saskia thought of the picture in Phil and Ruth's book, of the tall, harmless-looking old man with the strawberry mark on his face. Bad Jack Mackey would be in that lit room. Soon she'd be in it too.

There was a sort of shiver in the air beside her, and Birdie Murray was standing there.

'Well,' Birdie said softly, 'that's the aisy bit done. We dealt with the monkey, now for the organ-grinder.'

'Mrs Murray,' Saskia whispered, 'I think I'm afraid.'

Birdie Murray smiled at her. 'Good, so,' she said. 'I'd be more worried if you weren't.'

'I know this is a dream,' Saskia said. 'But I know that it isn't quite a dream too.'

Birdie Murray reached up and took off her little straw hat. She took several pins from her hair and it fell, astonishingly long, down around her shoulders, reaching almost to her waist.

'Indeed, it is a dream,' she said to Saskia, 'and it ain't a dream. It's betwixt and between, Saskia, like the place we are now. It's a game, but it's a very important one. Just like life. Are you ready?'

Saskia could feel herself starting to shiver. A bird began to sing in a tree nearby. She'd never heard a bird sing at night before. Birdie Murray looked sharply at the tree. The singing stopped in mid-note.

'Are you ready?' Birdie asked again.

The world seemed very still. 'Not really,' Saskia said. 'But I'll be no more ready if we wait. Go ahead.'

And then they were standing in a lamplit room, and Saskia knew it was the room whose light she'd seen through the curtains. It was an old-fashioned room, full of overstuffed furniture. There was a tall figure standing at a table with his back turned to them – Jack Mackey, Saskia knew. He was pouring whiskey into a tumbler. He turned and looked at Birdie Murray. He was smiling.

'Ah!' he said mildly. 'Me ould segotia! I knew you'd turn up one of these nights.'

'You know me, Jackie,' Birdie said. 'The proverbial bad penny.'

Jack Mackey didn't look evil or dangerous. He looked like somebody's grandfather. In this light the strawberry mark on his face didn't stand out. He gestured towards the table, where a tray of bottles and glasses stood.

'Will you have a drop, Livvie? Or is it Kitty now, or another? Why you bother with all of these names I'll never know.'

'You never did understand names, Jackie,' Birdie said. 'You hadn't the patience. My name is Birdie now. And no, I won't have anything.'

'Fair enough,' Jack Mackey said mildly. He took a sip from

136

his drink. 'I suppose,' he said, 'this means my Pooshipaw is ... gone?'

'Not a bit of it.'

'No?' For the first time the old man seemed vaguely put out. 'Not gone?'

'Sure I shook hands with him only a few minutes ago,' Birdie said.

Mackey looked positively dumbfounded. 'You shook ...'

Birdie held out her hand and shook an imaginary other hand. She gave a skeleton's grin and sketched a mocking curtsey. 'The right hand, don't you know, Jackie,' she said. 'That's how us polite people does it.'

'He crossed over,' Mackey said, thinlipped.

'He crossed over,' Birdie Murray agreed.

'I didn't know that could be done.'

'What you don't know, Jackie,' Birdie said, 'would fill a grand big book, so it would. It can be done and it can't be done. It depends on who's doing the doing, so to speak.'

Something like worry flickered across the old man's face. Then he just looked cross.

'It's not fair,' he said. 'Destruction is permitted, theft is not.'

'He done it of his own free will,' Birdie Murray said.

'Free will!' Jack Mackey looked as outraged as he sounded. 'In a Pooshipaw! Sure they've hardly a brain! You're getting soft in your ould age, woman. Or dangerous.'

'I was always dangerous, Jack,' Birdie purred. 'To the likes of you, at least.'

'And I to you,' Jack Mackey said coldly.

Saskia wondered why Mackey was ignoring her so completely. Maybe, she thought, it was simply contempt. He was looking closely at Birdie Murray, studying her. He began to walk around Birdie, not taking his eyes off her. Birdie turned slowly as Mackey walked, so that she kept facing him. Her arms were by her sides, one of them holding her little straw hat. The fingers of her free hand, Saskia saw, were stretched out clawlike, like a gunslinger in a cowboy film waiting to draw his gun. The tall old man walked towards Saskia without even looking at her, and she sucked in her breath in a gasp as he ... she didn't even know how to describe it to herself: one moment Bad Jack Mackey was about to bump into her, the next he was behind her. She'd felt nothing. She whirled around to look, but Mackey hadn't even noticed that he'd just walked right through her. And suddenly it dawned on Saskia that Bad Jack Mackey didn't know she was there.

'Lord, girlie,' Mackey said to Birdie Murray, 'but you've left it very late this time, haven't you? You're decrepit. Can't you even pin your hair up any more?'

'Don't,' Birdie Murray said warningly, 'call me girlie, ould man.'

'I recall,' Jack Mackey said, 'times you had flesh on them bones.'

'And I,' purred Birdie, 'recall times you'd no marks on your face.'

Mackey stopped walking. His face flushed. The strawberry stain grew livid in the dim room. It seemed almost to shine with a light of its own.

'So,' Birdie said, 'we're still sensitive about that, are we?'

For answer Jack Mackey made a hissing sound.

'Down all the dear dead years,' Birdie Murray said, 'down all the poor ould lives, you never left a mark on me that didn't go. But I left one on you, Jackie boy. Poor ould Birdie's bones left a big bad mark on big bad Jackie.' Her voice oozed a jeering contempt. It was an ugly sound. Phil should have heard this, Saskia thought, before he accused Birdie of jeering at him.

Saskia was actually looking at Jack Mackey when he moved, but he was so fast that she didn't see him do it. One moment he was standing easy with his glass in his left hand, the next the glass was falling and the same hand, palm outward, was directed at Birdie Murray. Something very hard to describe shot out of that palm. It was like a ray of dark light, like some kind of beam of blackness.

In the same instant Birdie Murray raised her old straw hat so that it caught the beam of almost-light, which disappeared into it without a trace. There was a faint bad smell in the air, very like the ghost-smell left behind by the Pooshipaw. Birdie grinned with her yellow teeth.

'Go to it, Jackie boy!' she urged. 'You'll have to do better nor that.'

Jack Mackey's whole face now was a blazing red. His other hand shot up, and another beam of dark light flashed at Birdie.

Birdie Murray drew herself up. She was smiling. She held her arms wide open, as though in welcome. Saskia's mouth fell open. The beam hit Birdie Murray full in the stomach, driving all the air out of her body in a great gasp. Her face twisted into an ugly rictus of pain. The force of the blow threw her back against the wall.

For an instant Saskia stood frozen with shock. She heard the sound of breaking glass, and saw that only now had Jack Mackey's tumbler hit the wooden floor – that was how quickly the whole thing had happened. In her shock Saskia dropped the pebble from her hand. Birdie Murray's body bounced off the wall and tumbled to the floor, like a broken bird that had flown into a window. Saskia screamed.

Bad Jack Mackey breathed deeply and looked at his old enemy lying on the ground. Then he turned slowly and looked straight at Saskia, his eyebrows raised in mild surprise. His eyes became happy. He smiled. It wasn't a nice smile.

'Well, well, well,' he said. 'And what have we here? Dessert?'

CURSES

Saskia grew very cold as the tall old stick of a man looked at her. His look was mild, but infinitely threatening. She wanted to run, but couldn't move. She tried desperately to think of anything she might do to this man, but nothing came to mind. How could she hope to hurt someone who had dealt so easily with Birdie Murray?

There was a groan from the body on the floor. Mackey looked over.

'I told you, girlie,' he said, 'you left it very late. You mix with these people too much. It's weakening to mingle with the weak. It rubs off on you.'

Saskia was amazed to see that Birdie Murray was moving. It was only a scrabbling of her hands and feet, but still you'd think that anyone of Birdie's age bounced in such a fashion off a wall would have been broken by the impact alone. Saskia wanted to run to the old woman, her own danger forgotten.

'I don't think so,' Jack Mackey said to her. 'You stay away from the ould biddy. I like her better like that, crawling on her own.' He grinned. 'Where are all your humans now,' he called over to Birdie, 'now that it's your turn to need a bit of help?'

'We're all human, Jackie,' Birdie Murray groaned. 'More or less.'

'Speak for yourself, woman,' Jack Mackey said, sounding offended. He stepped carefully over the spilled drink and broken glass on the floor and came over to Saskia. He saw the dropped stone on the floor and probed it carefully with his foot before picking it up and examining it.

'Well, well,' he said. 'An enchanted stone. How quaint. I haven't seen one of them in years.' He threw the stone on the ground and looked over at the struggling figure of Birdie Murray. 'I'm surprised at you, dear,' he said, 'using an ould cheap trick like an invisibility spell.'

'It worked all the same,' said Birdie Murray slowly, painfully, from the floor. 'Better nor you know. An ould cheap trick to fool an ould cheap man.' To Saskia's astonishment she had risen to her hands and knees, though her head was hanging and she groaned.

Jack Mackey walked over to Birdie Murray and stood over her with his hands on his hips, thinking. He gave a little smile. Then he drew back his foot and kicked her viciously in the side. Birdie collapsed with a deflated grunt.

Saskia screamed again. She had never witnessed anything so cruel. Jack Mackey looked over at her, rubbing his hands. He was smiling widely now.

'You go ahead and scream, dear,' he said in a silken purr. 'You scream as much as you want. It warms the cockles of my heart, so it does. It's like water to parched earth, like sweet music to my weary ould ears. And sure we'll have a regular concert later on, so we will, just you and me: once I've finished with this hag.'

His voice was positively genial. Suddenly Saskia wasn't afraid any more. Instead she was furious. This old man was nobody's grandfather. He was a monster. She let rip with a string of curses in Dutch and English such as she had never in her life said to anyone. She called Jack Mackey things that were unnatural, things she didn't even understand herself. She found herself using words she hadn't even known she knew. Mackey stood looking at her, his grin slowly fading. After a long while Saskia ran out of curses and started simply insulting him.

'Coward!' she said. 'Pig!'

Jack Mackey listened to her coldly. His smile had disappeared by now. His expression didn't grow angry, but his face grew slowly red again. The strawberry stain grew redder and darkened, from strawberry to purple, till it glowed almost black in the dim light.

'I hate a foul mouth on a child,' he said primly, when Saskia paused. 'If you won't use your tongue properly, my sweet, then maybe you'd be better off without it.'

'Bully!' Saskia hissed at him. She'd worked herself up to the point where she simply didn't care what he did to her. The sight of the pleasure on his face as he'd kicked Birdie had been the last straw.

'You'll do nothing to me,' she said. 'You wouldn't have the neck. Bullies never do. You've no Pooshipaw now to do your dirty work for you.'

Jack Mackey strode over and stood in front of her. His eyes bored into hers. He was as angry as she was.

'Nobody,' he said, 'talks to me like that! I need no Pooshipaw to do my work for me. I need nobody. You're in my house now, uninvited. The day you crossed my threshold will be the sorriest day of your miserable, feeble life. You're mine now. I have control over exactly how to hurt you – exactly how.'

Saskia was beyond caring. She still couldn't move, but she searched in her mind for the lowest insults she could think of. Some of her father's favourites came to mind.

'Politician!' she said. 'Critic!'

Jack Mackey's face was positively shining with supreme anger. He drew back his hand.

'Leave the child alone!' Birdie Murray said. The voice was firm and commanding. Jack Mackey froze where he was. Saskia stopped in mid-insult. Both of them looked over, but Birdie was still lying prone on the floor. Slowly, hesitantly, the broken old witch stretched out an arm. A thin finger pointed straight at Jack Mackey.

'My ould bones marked your face before, Jackie Mackey,' she said. 'If you so much as touch that girl, my ould bones will scald your black heart.'

Jack Mackey snorted. 'My dear,' he said to Birdie, 'you're not dealing with a Pooshipaw now.'

He reached out and took Saskia's chin in a fierce grip between his thumb and forefinger, twisting her face up towards him. The grip hurt. His fingers felt like metal bars. Saskia looked into his eyes – he was holding her so that she was forced to do so. He smiled thinly at her, saying nothing. His eyes were pools of black filth. Saskia began once again to be afraid. Unconsciously she clenched her fist hard on the bone she still held in her hand.

'The Pooshipaw,' she said coldly to Jack Mackey, 'is ten times the man you'll ever be.'

Jack Mackey's face went from red to white. His fingers tightened on her chin.

Saskia spat in his face. For a moment Jack Mackey seemed paralysed by sheer shock. Then he slapped her, very hard, with the open palm of his free hand. Saskia felt as though her head had exploded. There were spots in front of her eyes. Her ears rang. She made no sound, but felt the tears fall from her eyes.

'Ah,' Jack Mackey said, 'the good ould waterworks. A sight I love to see.' He leaned down and pulled her face viciously forward till it was just inches from his own. Saskia could see her spit still on his cheek. His eyes now were full of other people's nightmares. 'That was a foretaste, childeen,' he said. 'A foretaste.' He licked his lips.

'Ould bones, Jack,' said Birdie Murray, in a voice like something from the grave. 'Ould bones and your black heart! Saskia! My ould bone!'

And suddenly, in the midst of the pain and the shame and the fury, Saskia understood. She felt a shift in Jack Mackey, a sudden alertness. But he was distracted by his fury. Saskia shifted the old bone in her hand till it stuck up from her clenched fist like a blade. With a single short movement she drew back her arm and stabbed the bone at Bad Jack Mackey's chest. She could not miss.

The bone was old, stubby, and dull. It could never have wounded anyone. But when it hit Jack Mackey's chest Saskia felt a great concussion. She and Mackey were thrown apart, his fingers ripped from her chin. Saskia was flung to the floor. She saw something like a flash of light, heard what she thought of as a hollow, sucking sound.

Saskia lay stunned. She had no idea whether she lay there for seconds or minutes. The whole room seemed to hum, with a sound like struck crystal. She was roused from her daze by the last sound on earth she'd expected to hear. It was the sound of Birdie Murray chuckling.

SUMO WRESTLERS

When Saskia sat up she saw Bad Jack Mackey still lying on the floor. His arms were flung wide. He was breathing, but his eyes were closed. There was a mark like a burn on his chest where the bone had struck. The cloth of his waistcoat was singed and smoking. A faint sort of haze seemed to hang around his body, but when Saskia tried to focus on it properly she couldn't see any haze at all.

Birdie Murray continued to chuckle. When Saskia dragged her eyes away from Bad Jack she saw that Birdie was sitting up as well. She was supporting herself against the wall, and her face was white. When she saw that Saskia was looking at her she shook her head.

'Begob, girl,' she said, 'you'll never win any prizes for taking hints, will you? I had to nearly spell it out for you.'

Saskia got shakily to her feet. Her cheeks were still wet with the tears she'd cried. Her jaw felt numb where Mackey's steel fingers had clamped it.

'Mrs Murray!' she said. 'Are you all right?'

Birdie Murray leaned back against the wall. 'Well, I wouldn't go so far as to say I was all right,' she said. 'I'm damned sore, for one thing, and I think I'm a bit broke up inside. But I've been worse in me time, believe you me.'

'Do you need a doctor?'

At this Birdie Murray laughed hard. Then she groaned. 'Girleen, girleen,' she said, 'don't make me laugh like that.'

Saskia had spoken without thinking. She realised her own foolishness. To a doctor – if she could find one – they'd both look like ghosts if they could be seen at all. Then again, in some ways this was a dream, and the Birdie that was hurt might not be the real physical Birdie.

'What about Bad Jack?' she asked Birdie. The old man hadn't stirred.

Birdie by now was pulling herself to her feet. 'Poor ould Jackser,' she said, 'lost again.'

She came painfully over and stood looking down at Jack Mackey. She shook her head. 'Pure vanity and bull-necked pride,' she said. 'Again. Ah well! With any luck the ould goat will never learn.'

Saskia was beginning to recover from her shock a little bit. 'Mrs Murray?' she said. 'What exactly did I do?'

'Lord, girl,' Birdie said, 'sure you hit him with the bone, didn't you?'

'But did you plan that all along?'

'Don't be daft, girl – how could I plan it? But the chance turned up, and I couldn't very well do it, could I? You had the bone in your hand, not me.'

She had that mild tone in her voice which Saskia had heard before. She suspected that it was a tone Birdie used when she was lying.

'Away with you, girl,' Birdie Murray said. 'You're too suspicious.'

'That second thing he threw at you,' Saskia said. 'That ... bolt of energy, or whatever it was ...'

'It's as good a name as any.'

'You let it hit you. You did it on purpose.'

'I did, bedad. He wasn't expecting that. That's when we started to win, do you see.'

'No, I don't see,' Saskia said, almost crossly.

Birdie Murray looked oddly at her. 'Do you know,' she said, 'you're starting to sound like your uncle Phil.'

That made Saskia pause, and she suspected Birdie Murray had meant it to.

'Don't expect me,' Birdie said, 'to stand here and explain our rules to you, because I can't. They're not them kind of rules. But I'll tell you this – you mentioned Japan today.'

'Yes. My father's very interested in Japan.'

'Did you ever see them wrestlers they haves over there? Sumo wrestlers?'

'Yes. I've seen them on television.'

'Well, think of that, then, if you don't know what you're looking at. You sees these two big boyos getting into a ring. Two big haycocks of men. They looks at one another a bit, they walks around one another a bit, and next thing one of them's flat on his back and the match is over. Do you see?'

'Yes, but it's not like that, is it? It's all about one of them getting the other off-balance, striking at exactly the right second.'

'It is, it is! That's exactly what it is! And that's very like the way it is with me and Jack when we fights. Did you ever see a sumo wrestler giving another one a box in the jaw?'

'Of course not. It's not allowed.'

'No, it's not. It's against the rules. Well, when Jackie kicked me tonight, that was against the rules too. But when he slapped you, he threw the rule book out the window altogether. Jackie is not let get physical, do you see? That's why you could hit him with the bone.'

Saskia shook her head. 'But he hit me because I got him angry,' she said. 'Because I cursed him.'

'And a fine cursing it was. There was a few words there

you must teach me sometime. But you cursed him because he kicked me.'

'But he must know the rules as well as you do. He must have known then that he shouldn't kick you.'

'Ah, but he had a bit of prompting there.'

'He did?'

'He thought the stone was to make you invisible to him, do you see.'

'Wasn't it? He didn't see me till I dropped it.'

'It was for that, right enough, but there was more in it too.'

'What?' demanded Saskia.

'A little sup of Phil's annoyance, just to make Jackie that bit more foolhardy. That was in the stone as well.'

Saskia was trying to make sense of this when something else struck her. 'He only saw the stone,' she said, 'because I dropped it. And I dropped it from shock when that beam of whatever-it-was hit you. And you let it hit you on purpose.'

Birdie Murray smiled. 'There we are back at that again,' she said. 'Ain't it nice when things are neat?'

'You knew it all!' Saskia said. 'You did plan it! Didn't you?'

'Hush, childeen,' Birdie Murray said. 'Sure how could I plan all of that? Talk sense.'

'But this is sense,' Saskia said. 'You wanted me to be the one to get Bad Jack Mackey! Why did you do that to me?'

Birdie wasn't smiling any more. 'Child,' she said calmly, 'you're a bit shocked. You wouldn't ask so many questions otherwise. If I did anything tonight then I did something for you, not *to* you. And you did something for me. And for Simon. And for yourself.'

Birdie wasn't just talking about hitting Bad Jack Mackey, Saskia knew; she realised that most things the old woman did and said worked on two levels at least.

'What was it I did?' she asked Birdie.

'You crossed over, just a little bit,' Birdie Murray said. It was the phrase she'd used to Mackey about the Pooshipaw. Saskia started to ask what it meant, but Birdie held up a silencing hand.

'You wanted wild dreams, love,' she said gently. She gestured around at the room, at the old man on the floor, at the finger bone which Saskia only now saw she was still holding.

'This is a damn good start, don't you think?' Birdie said.

NEW TOYS

The alarm clock was set for half-past six in the morning, but Ruth and Phil woke up before it went off. Both of them were wide awake at once, but each lay for a moment thinking that the other was asleep.

'Phil?' said Ruth then.

Her husband grunted. He reached up and switched off the alarm. Then they looked at each other.

Phil licked his lips nervously. 'Did he wake in the night?' he asked. 'Did I sleep through anything?'

'You must be joking! Do you think I'd have let you? I did wake up, though. There was a fire someplace, and the sirens woke me. I got a real fright, but when I saw it wasn't our house on fire I just went to sleep again.'

They both turned and looked at the winking red light of the baby intercom. The sound of Simon's clock ticked and tocked from his room. That was all.

'Phil,' Ruth admitted, 'I'm scared to look in.'

Phil sighed. 'So am I,' he said. 'But we'll look anyway.'

They tiptoed to the door of Simon's room. Phil put his hand on the handle. Then he stopped and looked at his wife.

'We'll do this together,' he said.

Ruth's nod was short and brave. 'Together,' she said.

Phil opened the door. They went in.

The curtains were closed and the room was still half-dark, but the little night lamp threw light on the bed. Simon was lying on his back with his arms and legs thrown wide. He'd pushed his duvet off. He was breathing sweetly and evenly, and his face was lit up with the brightest, widest smile that either Phil or Ruth had ever seen there. They knew with an absolute certainty, as though someone had spoken the words to them, that their son was fine – that he was better than fine, if there was such a thing.

Then Ruth sniffed the air. 'What's that smell?' she whispered.

Phil sniffed. 'What smell?'

'It was like ... I don't know. Like flowers. It's gone now.'

Phil put his arm around her shoulders. They stood looking down at Simon. Then Ruth looked around the room.

'Phil?' she said. 'What's that?'

She went over and picked something up from the foot of the bed.

'Ugh!' she said.

It was Tiger Mike. Only now there was something else, a second figure sitting astride the tiger's back.

'Good God!' Phil said. 'What's that?'

The figure on the tiger's back was like nothing that they'd ever seen before. It was a stuffed animal, certainly, but it didn't look like any animal they knew. It was a squat, dumpy, furry thing, dressed in a battered derby hat and what looked like a dirty raincoat with no arms. The creature had big round eyes of a pale yellow colour, and a huge grinning mouth that showed the tips of fangs.

'Is it a cat?' Phil said. 'Or a dog?'

'All I know,' Ruth said, 'is that it doesn't belong here.'

She tried to pull the creature off the tiger's back, but it wouldn't come. Tiger Mike's face smiled blankly up at her as she pulled.

'Phil?' Ruth said. She held the two figures up towards him. 'Stuck?'

'It's not just stuck, Phil. It's like they're made all of a piece!'

'But that can't be! It's twenty years and more since I got Tiger Mike!' He took Tiger Mike in one hand and the ugly new creature in the other. Then he pulled. Nothing happened.

'Phil!' Ruth said. She'd seen something else on the ground beside the bed. She picked it up. It was a toy car, an old-fashioned thing with spoked wheels and high seats and a cloth hood like a buggy. It was a bright emerald colour.

'The green car!' Phil whispered.

Simon woke up.

'MammyDaddy!' he said, excited. 'MammyDaddy!'

He sat up in bed.

'Simon?' Ruth said. 'Are you all right?'

Simon grinned at her. Ruth felt her question had been foolish. The child glowed with health and happiness.

'No bad dreams, boyo?' Phil asked.

Simon shook his head. 'Good dreams,' he said. 'Very good dreams. With Tiger Mike and Saskia and Auntie Birdie.'

Then he saw the car in Ruth's hands, and the two joined creatures in Phil's.

'The green car!' he said. 'And look, look – the Pooshipaw!'

Phil nearly dropped the stuffed toys. He looked down, horrified, at the ugly thing sitting on Mike's back. Simon saw the look of horror on his face.

'It's all right, Daddy,' he said. 'The Pooshipaw is Simon's friend now.'

Phil said the sort of very rude word that he always tried not to say in front of Simon. 'Sorry, love,' he said to Ruth. 'It just sort of slipped out.'

But Ruth hadn't even noticed. She too was staring at the new toy, or the new part of the old toy, or whatever it really was.

'Phil,' she said, 'we have to get rid of that thing!'

'No, no, Mammy,' Simon corrected her. 'The Pooshipaw lives here now. Auntie Birdie says. He'll mind us. He's a good boy now. He was lonely before.'

Phil looked at the ugly thing. 'Lonely?' he said. 'I'm not surprised.'

'I thought this Pooshipaw thing was supposed to be malformed,' Ruth said. 'He was supposed to have his head where his heart should be or something.'

'It was his hands,' Simon said. 'Auntie Birdie fixed it.'

Phil and Ruth looked at each other. Then Phil looked again at the creature, at its big grin.

'It will never be pretty,' he said. 'That grin looks positively sinister.'

Simon was standing on tiptoe, looking at the animals in his Daddy's hands. He stroked the Pooshipaw's head, then looked seriously up at Phil's face. 'That's his first smile,' he said. 'He has to learn, Auntie Birdie says.'

'Auntie Birdie says,' Phil repeated. 'That's the law around here these days.'

Simon pulled the animals from his hand and hugged them. 'It's a good law,' he said. He leaned down and whispered into what Phil supposed must be the Pooshipaw's ear. It was hard to tell with all that fur.

Saskia came into the room. She was yawning and smiling at once.

'Saskia,' Ruth said. 'Simon's all right! It's over!'

'Yes,' said her niece. She didn't sound at all surprised. 'Isn't it wonderful?'

Phil looked at her suspiciously. 'He said you were there,' he said. 'Simon said that you and Mike and Birdie Murray were there.'

Saskia gave him a look of surprise at once so innocent and false that it put him in mind of Birdie Murray.

'I was in my bed,' she said. 'Dreaming dreams.'

'About Pooshipaws?'

She grinned in a very strange way. 'I dreamed about lots of things last night,' she said. Then she bent to kiss Simon good morning. Simon giggled, and Phil was almost certain that he caught Saskia winking at the child. Then she turned towards the door. 'You two look distracted,' she said. 'I'll make breakfast.'

Phil glared after her when she left. Again he had the feeling that everyone knew what was going on except himself and Ruth. But then Simon laughed again, and he thought who cared what was going on? Simon was all right – of that much at least he felt sure.

Ruth opened the curtains. Light flooded into the room. It was a beautiful morning, not a cloud in the sky.

'I'm not going to work,' she said. 'Not today.'

'No,' Phil said. 'Neither am I.'

'We'll get in trouble,' Ruth said.

Phil shrugged. 'Trouble,' he said, 'is relative. I think we deserve a day to get used to this.'

Simon was still stroking the Pooshipaw and Tiger Mike. Phil reached down and ruffled his son's hair.

'What do you say, kid?' he asked. 'Fancy going to the park with Mammy and Daddy?'

'And Saskia and Tiger Mike and the Pooshipaw,' Simon said.

Phil sighed. 'And Saskia and Tiger Mike,' he said. 'And ... the Pooshipaw.'

Simon nodded. 'We've the best Daddy,' he said confidentially to the Pooshipaw. 'And the best Mammy. We're lucky boys.'

'The park won't be open yet,' Ruth said. She felt a need to be practical.

'So what?' Phil said. He felt a need to be impractical. People do the same thing in different ways. 'We'll climb over the fence. I fancy a go on a slide.'

Ruth giggled. Phil smiled. Simon laughed.

After breakfast they drove up towards the park. Saskia sat in the back with Simon, who cradled Tiger Mike and the Pooshipaw in his lap. Every now and again the two children would look at each other and giggle. Even Phil found that he didn't mind.

When they got near the park they saw the dark smoke hanging in the air behind the trees. Ruth suddenly remembered the sirens she'd heard in the night.

'Phil?' she said. 'That house. The place we bought the bed ...'

'It must be just back there,' Phil said.

'Stay away,' Ruth said, but Phil said he had to see.

They drove towards the source of the smoke. It was, indeed, the old house where they'd bought the bed. The fire-engine was still there, but the firemen were getting ready to go. There were two police cars, and an unmarked car full of men who looked like plainclothes policemen trying not to look like plainclothes policemen.

'Keep moving, please,' a uniformed officer said to Phil when he stopped. Phil kept driving, slowly. But they'd already seen the house. As they drove on, no-one said anything. Then Saskia and Simon giggled again. The adults both shivered at the sound.

The old house was a smoking ruin. The roof was gone, and the walls were blackened stumps. Even the garden and the hedges were black and smoking. It looked as though a bomb had hit it, a very big bomb. Outside of the hedges, though, nothing was even damaged.

'Nothing came out of that house alive,' Phil said darkly.

'It's all right, Daddy,' came a small, happy voice from the back. When they looked back Simon was grinning at them. He held up Tiger Mike and the Pooshipaw. 'There was nothing alive in the house,' Simon said. 'It was only Bad Jack, and Bad Jack ...' He seemed to be struggling for words. Then he seemed to hear something. He held the Pooshipaw up to his ear and seemed to listen. Then he nodded happily and looked up smiling at his Mammy and Daddy. 'Bad Jack just isn't,' he said. 'Not any more. Auntie Birdie took him.'

Then he looked at Saskia, and the two of them giggled again. Phil stopped the car. He stared for a long time, first at Simon and then at Saskia. He noticed too that odd marks like bruises were coming up on either side of Saskia's face. They were almost the shape of fingers.

'What happened to your face, Saskia?' Phil asked finally.

Saskia raised a hand to stroke her chin. 'It's silly, really,' she said. 'I was having this mad dream this morning and I fell out of bed. Cracked my chin on the bedside table. Does it look bad?'

'No,' Phil said. 'I just wondered.'

Then he looked at Simon again, and then back at Saskia. They both looked innocently back at him. Just for a change Phil looked at Tiger Mike, and then at the grinning figure of the Pooshipaw, but they looked just as innocent. Finally he shrugged.

'For just this once,' he said, 'I don't even want to know. Let's go to the park.'

AUDITORS OUT

'The surf at La Jolla is better,' Tiger Mike said. 'Tube city, man.'

'Be off with you, then, to La Jolla!' said the Pooshipaw. 'You mangy big lug.'

'Gee,' said Mike, 'I didn't mean anything! You really are touchy sometimes, you know that?'

'Rubbish,' said the Pooshipaw. 'I'm just fed up with your carping.'

Simon laughed. He enjoyed these spats. Tiger Mike and the Pooshipaw were getting along very well, but neither one of them wanted to admit it.

The three of them were sitting on a golden beach the Pooshipaw had made. The beach was in a little cove. Great waves made of apple-juice pounded the yellow sand, throwing a fine, cooling spray over the three friends. The foam on the waves was made of whipped cream. It was very warm on the beach. The sun was high in the sky.

Now that he had hands like everyone else, the Pooshipaw decided to take up playing the guitar. Unfortunately, while he could make a guitar from nothing, he couldn't make himself know how to play. He had to learn, like anyone else, and he didn't really have the patience for such pursuits. He was strumming on his guitar now, jangling discords that made Tiger Mike grind his great teeth.

Still, Mike was determined to be friendly. 'Anyhow,' he said, 'the waves at La Jolla don't taste as good as these. This is pretty excellent work, dude.'

The Pooshipaw just grunted. He wasn't used to compliments. He was getting quite a few of them these days, though, and was coming to like them – though he'd never admit that either.

The Pooshipaw was beginning to like places that weren't dirty, too, though that was still another thing he wouldn't admit. But Simon and Mike both noticed how carefully he kept the lovely guitar he'd made. He didn't exactly clean it, but he made any dirt or grease that got on it simply disappear. He might never learn to play the guitar, but at least it would always look good.

To Mike's relief now the Pooshipaw laid the guitar down on the sand. He settled back and sighed, and held out his good right hand. A long drink in a frosted glass appeared in it. 'I'd like to see you do better, at any rate,' he said to Mike.

But Mike was distracted. He sniffed the air. 'Hey, man,' he said to Simon. 'You're near your Nanny's. You'd better start waking up.'

'Okay,' Simon said. 'See you later.'

The Pooshipaw sucked noisily at his drink. He still had a lot to learn about table manners, but then he had lots of time.

'Tonight, Sausage,' he said. 'We'll try this snowman-building lark. I'll make the mountain out of chocolate, and I think I've got the taste right for the ice-cream for the snow. And Saskia will be there. This big housecat here is going to teach her to ski.'

'Say hello to your Nanny for me,' Tiger Mike told Simon, and went back to building his sandcastle.

Simon opened his eyes with a smile. He was in his child-seat in the back of the car. In the driver's mirror he saw his Mammy's eyes smiling back at him.

'He's awake, Phil,' Ruth said. 'And still smiling.'

'Honestly,' Phil said. 'There was never a child so happy to sleep as he is nowadays. We'll be worrying about that next.'

'No!' said Ruth, very definitely, and then she laughed.

They were almost at Nanny's house. It was Friday evening, the weekend after Birdie Murray had visited them. They'd put Saskia on a plane to Amsterdam the night before. She'd been sorry to go, and they'd been sorry she was going.

'I meant to take the other road,' Phil said now. 'I wanted to go by the graveyard. I want to take a look in there.'

'For what?'

'For graves.'

'Livvie Crowe's?'

'Livvie Crowe's, Kitty Mahon's ... who knows how many more?'

'I think we should leave it alone,' Ruth said. She wasn't laughing now. 'I think we got off very lightly in this. I don't think it's our business. When Birdie wouldn't answer questions, she was trying to protect us. Even knowing might be dangerous.'

'Still, you can't help being curious.'

'Yes I can,' Ruth said. She was deadly serious. 'I stopped being curious the minute I saw that house – what was left of it. And I want you to stop being curious too.'

They turned the corner and saw Nanny's gate.

'There's Ma going in,' Phil said.

Nanny hadn't noticed the car. Phil beeped the horn as he turned into the yard. His mother was standing there, smiling and waving at them. She was dressed very formally, and she was wearing a hat. Ruth didn't really notice, but Phil had been brought up here and he saw it straight away.

'Something's wrong,' he said as he parked the car. He rolled down the window. 'Ma?' he said.

Nanny seemed cheerful enough. 'Hello there,' she said.

In the back of the car Simon started cheering. Nanny smiled in at him. 'There's my boy,' she said.

She saw Tiger Mike and the Pooshipaw. Simon was holding them up to the window and telling the Pooshipaw who she was. Nanny wrinkled her nose.

'So that's the brute,' she said. 'God, he's ugly. Sure that yoke'd give anyone a bad dream! Still, I'm told he's harmless enough now.'

Phil and Ruth got out of the car. 'Ma,' Phil said, 'you look like you're coming from a funeral.'

'No,' Nanny said. 'Tonight was the removal to the chapel. The funeral's not till tomorrow. I'm glad you're here for it.'

'Who is it?' Phil said. A sudden terrible suspicion was born in him.

'Why, poor Birdie Murray,' Nanny said.

'Oh, no,' Ruth said. 'No.'

Nanny looked at them. 'Oh, it's sad enough,' she said. 'But sure she had a long life. When it's your time to go, you know, it's your time.'

Phil and Ruth were shocked by the news. Ruth thought Nanny was taking it very casually, that she was even being a bit heartless.

'I've no tea ready for youse,' Nanny said. 'But get your stuff in now and I'll get something organised. I baked a cake earlier.'

But Ruth and Phil were still dazed. 'What happened?' Phil asked. 'How did she die?'

'Who, Birdie? She was got dead in the bed this morning. It was a very peaceful death, thank God. She had a big smile on her face, I'm told. She looked like she was after being laid out already.'

Phil's mind was full of questions, so many that he couldn't think which to ask first. Nanny looked at him. 'Will youse get your stuff inside,' she said almost impatiently. 'Then we can talk.'

Ruth and Phil obeyed automatically. They were just down for the weekend and had only a few bags, mostly Simon's things. They took them from the boot and brought them in.

'What are we going to tell Simon?' Ruth whispered to Phil. 'He'll take this very hard. He's been talking all week about seeing his Auntie Birdie!'

They left the bags in the hall and went into the kitchen. Phil sat down weakly at the table. Through the window he saw his mother open the back door of the car and take Simon out of his seat. Simon still held tightly to Tiger Mike and the Pooshipaw. He threw his arms around his Nanny's neck and covered her face in kisses. 'I'm licking you!' they heard him shout, laughing.

'I don't know what we'll tell him,' Phil admitted. 'How can a three-year-old understand dying?'

'We'd have had to try explaining it sometime,' Ruth said. 'But it could have come at a better time. I'm still not over this Pooshipaw business.'

'It's not just Simon,' Phil said. 'I feel almost cheated. I had a few things to ask Birdie myself.'

Ruth filled the kettle and plugged it in, more to have something to do than anything else. They heard Simon's running feet in the hall. He was whooping his usual I'm-in-Nanny's whoop.

Phil sighed. 'Oh Lord,' he said. 'This is a shambles, isn't it?'

RUTH MAKES TEA

Simon came into the kitchen carrying Tiger Mike and the Pooshipaw. 'This is Nanny's kitchen,' he told the Pooshipaw.

Ruth and Phil exchanged miserable looks. Which of them was going to try explaining to him? Ruth sighed. 'Simon?' she said. 'Si?'

But Simon was busy. He was showing the Pooshipaw the kettle. 'It's like at home,' he explained. 'It's very hot sometimes. Very dangerous for little boys.'

Phil reached out and pulled Simon gently over to his chair. He put his hands on his son's shoulders. Simon stood between his knees looking up at him. His face was bright.

'Simon,' Phil said.

'The Pooshipaw likes Nanny's house, Daddy,' Simon said. 'He says it feels nice.'

'Si,' Phil said, 'we have some very sad news.'

But suddenly Simon wriggled under his hands. He was looking over towards the window. His nose wiggled as though he were smelling something. 'It's Auntie Birdie, Daddy!' he said excitedly. 'Auntie Birdie!'

'Why yes, it is,' Phil said, wondering how Simon knew. But then he realised Simon hadn't even been listening. He'd wriggled free now and run out of the room.

'This is going to be even harder than I thought,' Phil said.

Ruth was standing by the window, waiting for the kettle to boil. 'Who's that your mother's talking to?' she asked.

Phil got up and looked out. His mother was standing by the gate with a girl who looked like a teenager. The girl had long hair. She was dressed in a plaid shirt much too big for her and a pair of black jeans. Her hair hung down to her shoulders from a big flat cap on her head. Her face was vaguely familiar.

'Some kid from the village, I guess,' he said. He was thinking about time, about life and death and changes. 'I don't know any of the young people here any more,' he said. 'It's weird, though, how the faces stay the same. Sometimes I see kids hardly older than Simon in the street here and I can tell what family they're from.'

'Hmmm?' Ruth said. She was distracted.

'Things stay more the same down the country,' Phil said. 'Old things stay longer.'

'Like what? Like satellite television and computers?' Ruth hated finding rural pubs that were showing some satellite sports channel.

'That's just the surface,' Phil said. He was feeling very thoughtful. 'I mean things like the Birdie Murrays of this world. There's a sort of continuity.'

'A very long one in Birdie's case,' Ruth said. She was spooning tea-leaves into Nanny's china teapot. She liked to do very ordinary things in a crisis. It helped her to get used to things.

The kettle boiled. Ruth picked up the teapot. Poor Birdie!

she thought. Gone in her turn, like Livvie Crowe, like Kitty Mahon, like ... suddenly Ruth froze. A strange idea had struck her. 'Phil?' she said.

There was no answer. Ruth looked up. Her husband was staring out the window with a very peculiar look on his face.

Simon had run out to the gate and was standing with Nanny and the girl. He started jumping up and down, waving Tiger Mike and the Pooshipaw at the girl and shouting something at her.

Phil stared very hard at the girl. Then he said a very bad word. Then he said several more. He didn't apologise.

'Phil?' Ruth said. 'What is it?'

But Phil had taken off. He ran out of the kitchen as quickly as Simon had done just before him. Ruth was left staring at the empty doorway.

When Phil got outside the teenager had gone, and Nanny was coming back towards the house carrying Simon. She had a big smile on her face.

'Ma?' Phil said. 'Who was that girl?'

His mother didn't seem to hear. She walked right by him into the hall. Simon was laughing in her arms. Phil looked once at the gate, then followed them in. 'Ma?' he said.

'God bless the child,' Nanny said, 'but she's taking it very well. It must have been a shock for her all the same: her last relative in the world gone. Still, she's had hardship before. There she is, only a slip of a girl, and she's a widow already. She must've married very young.'

'Mammy?' Phil said.

Nanny put Simon down and started taking off her hat and coat. Ruth was in the kitchen doorway. She was still holding the teapot. Simon was doing his very happy hop, which was quite like his happy hop except that it was that bit madder. Nanny turned to Phil.

'Yes, son?' she asked. 'What were you asking me?'

'Who was that girl?'

'Sure that's Mary Wickham,' Nanny said.

'And who's she when she's at home?'

Nanny chuckled. 'That's a funny way of putting it,' she said. 'But I suppose she is at home now. She wants to stay here, anyhow.'

'Mammy!' Phil said impatiently.

'MammyDaddy!' Simon was calling happily. 'MammyDaddyNanny! MammyDaddyNannyBirdie!'

Nanny looked at Phil with a puzzled face. 'But of course that's right,' she said. 'You wouldn't know her at all. I only know her a few hours myself, but it feels like I've known her for years. She's a lovely young one.'

Phil breathed out very slowly. It as a thing he did when he needed patience, though it didn't always work. 'Mother,' he said. 'Please!'

Nanny still looked puzzled. 'Mary,' she began, 'is a sort of a niece of Birdie Murray's ...'

She got no further. 'Holy Mother of God!' Ruth said from the doorway. Phil turned back to the front door.

'Son?' Nanny said innocently, but her son was already gone. He ran straight to the gate and looked out. The girl was well down the road by now, walking along and wheeling a very high bicycle that could only be Birdie Murray's old high nellie. Phil wanted to call out to her, but his voice seemed to stick in his throat. He could only stand there with his mouth open and watch the girl walking away.

When she reached the bend in the road the girl stopped. She turned and looked back. It was too far away for him to make out her features, but he knew for certain that she saw him standing there. She raised one arm and waved at him. In the bright evening sun, Phil saw a quick flash of white teeth as she grinned. Then she climbed up on the high bike, rode around the bend and was gone.

Phil stood there for a little while looking at the empty road. Then he went back inside. Ruth was still standing in the kitchen doorway with the teapot forgotten in her hand. Her face was pale and blank.

'MammyDaddyNannyBirdie!' Simon said, and hopped off into the house.

Phil stared at his mother. She smiled back at him sweetly. From somewhere off in the house he heard Simon's voice introducing the Pooshipaw to his bed. 'This is Simon's Nanny-house bed,' he was saying. 'It's very cosy and warm. Bed, this is the Pooshipaw. Say hello, Pooshipaw!'

For just one moment Phil could have sworn that he heard a low, grumpy voice growling hello. He looked at Nanny with a face as white and blank as Ruth's.

'Rrrshhr?' he said.

'Did you miss Mary, then?' Nanny said. 'Sure what harm. You'll see her at the funeral, maybe. I'm delighted she's staying here. Birdie left her all her property, you know. You'd be surprised how much she had stashed away.'

Phil found his voice. 'Nothing about Birdie Murray,' he said very slowly and very deliberately, 'would surprise me in the slightest. I'm starting to think that nothing at all will ever surprise me again.'

'I'm sure you'll both like Mary Wickham,' Nanny said. 'You especially, Philip. You'll have lots to talk about with her.'

'Oh?' Phil said.

'Oh aye. She was in your line of work.'

'My line of work,' Phil said.

'Yes indeed. She used to work for a firm of auditors.'

'Auditors,' Phil said.

Looking at her husband's face, Ruth suddenly, for no good reason, wanted to laugh out loud. It felt like a very normal urge, and she'd been feeling a terrible longing for normality. 'I'll finish making the tea,' she said.

'The tea,' said Phil.

'Oh, shut up, Phil,' she laughed.

Her husband gave her a blank look.

'Shut up, Phil,' he said.

Ruth took a last scornful look at him and went into the kitchen. Simon was still off somewhere in the house, loudly venting his glee. As she picked up the kettle, Ruth started to hum. She was smiling.

'You know, May,' she said to Nanny, 'myself and Phil should really spend more time down here.'

She was really looking forward to meeting Mary Wickham.

SASKIA'S PLAN

They were spending the night on a houseboat belonging to one of her parents' friends; the next day they were going to Utrecht, where another friend was loaning them an apartment for the rest of the summer.

Saskia's bed was in a tiny cabin at the front of the houseboat. The bed took up most of the room, but it was only for a night and anyway she didn't mind. It was another new experience.

There was a little round window beside the bed, and Saskia had opened it to look out. The waters of the Amstel river plopped and sucked a few inches below her. The lights of Amsterdam, heavy with hints of adventure, spread out above. She was sorry they wouldn't be staying here longer, because it was one of the few cities she'd seen that she really liked. But she could always come back; it was only a half-hour by train from Utrecht. And she'd live here some day, she knew.

'It's a madhouse,' her father always said, explaining why he liked Amsterdam himself. Uncle Phil and Aunt Ruth had spent a weekend in the city once, and for years afterwards Phil never tired of saying what an awful place it was: 'Full of weirdos', as he put it.

Saskia smiled, thinking about her uncle. She doubted that he'd be so free with talk of weirdness in the future. In the long run, she thought, this whole experience might be good for him. Her father always said that life was about enlarging your ideas; well, Phil had just had his ideas enlarged, in spite of himself. Her own ideas had grown a bit too.

'You're looking well. So you didn't die of boredom, then?' her mother had joked at Schipol airport when she met her from the plane.

'Not at all,' Saskia told her. 'It was the most exciting time I had in ages.'

And her mother, no matter how hard she tried, couldn't find any sarcasm in her voice.

'Well in that case,' she said, 'either Ruth and Phil have changed or you have. I hope it's them.'

'It's all of us, really,' Saskia said. 'I'm growing up, and they're growing down. We're sort of meeting in the middle sometimes now.'

Her mother had stopped still and looked at her carefully.

'God help us,' she'd said. 'You sound more like your father all the time.' But she hadn't sounded displeased at the idea.

On the houseboat now Saskia closed the little window, mindful of the mosquitoes that might be out on this sticky summer night. Was it still water they liked, or flowing? She could never remember. She lay on her back on the bed and stretched lazily, looking up at the low ceiling, thinking of Phil and Ruth, and Simon and his Nanny, and Birdie Murray and Tiger Mike, and of the Pooshipaw. She'd been thinking quite a lot about Pooshipaws, actually.

She'd sworn to Phil that she knew nothing about what actually happened last Sunday night. She knew that he didn't believe her, though he hadn't pressed her about it.

'I know by the look on your face that I'll get nothing out of you,' he'd muttered. 'It's the look that Ruth gets when she's lying through her teeth. And your mother too, for that matter. It obviously runs in the family.'

In a way Saskia felt he was only muttering from habit. In the days after Sunday she'd seen a real change in Phil, a willingness just to accept things. He'd been ... almost fun, really. Certainly far less dull. One day he'd even gone to work without a tie. And he really did look quite handsome when he relaxed. There was life in his face. A couple of times Saskia had almost wanted to tell him about Sunday night, at least about the ride in the green car. Not the rest of it, though – that was private.

But Birdie had warned her to say nothing to anyone about any of Sunday night's events. And really in a sort of a way what she'd told Phil was quite true: she knew nothing for sure. The bruises on her face had faded after a couple of days, though even now sometimes she felt a twinge in the bone where Jack Mackey's fingers had clamped on her chin. And as time passed the intensity of the whole thing had faded too, and the details had blurred at the edges a bit. She was just that bit too old now, Birdie had warned her: that world could not stay as real for her as it had been on that night. For Saskia now the whole thing really had been a sort of a dream, although a very vivid one.

'But sure it's all a dream, love,' Birdie had explained to her that day at her cottage. 'The place where the Pooshipaw lives is the Pooshipaw's dream, and the place where we lives is our dream. All the worlds are only dreams we all makes up between us.'

Saskia thought that was a lovely idea. It sounded like something her father might say. She was sorry now that her father hadn't met Birdie Murray; she was sure they'd have a lot to talk about.

From the deck of the houseboat she could hear her parents talking and laughing with the owners of the boat. She heard wineglasses clinking and jazz playing softly from the stereo. The music was by Thelonius Monk: you could tell his piano-playing a mile away. Her father played Monk a lot while he was painting.

'Listen to Monk,' he'd advised her once, 'and you'll hear the world laughing at itself.'

So Saskia had listened to Monk, and sometimes, yes, she could hear the echoes of that laughter. It sounded a bit like Birdie Murray's. She wondered whether Birdie had ever heard Monk. Maybe she'd ask her. She imagined the old woman saying, 'Sure didn't I mind him and he a babby?' Saskia would only be mildly surprised. At the cottage that day – in between discussing dreams and monsters – Birdie had chatted a lot about Phil's family and the history of the village. Every person she mentioned seemed to have been in her care as an infant. And when Saskia had mentioned a film star she liked, Birdie had shocked her with the news that his family had often spent holidays in the area years before.

'They used to rent that cottage up the lane there,' Birdie said. 'I used to mind him betimes and he hardly crawling.'

'Mrs Murray,' Saskia said, 'to hear you talk you must have minded the whole world "and it a babby".'

Birdie Murray had fixed her with her flinty eyes, and then grinned with her yellow teeth. 'Childeen,' she'd said, 'sure that's what me and my kind are here for. Do you think the world is not a babby still?'

But Saskia hadn't felt ready yet to judge the world's maturity.

'The world never grows up,' Birdie told her. 'People does. Sometimes they grows up too much – like your uncle Phil.'

'And what happens to them then?'

Birdie Murray, sitting in the sunshine, had shrugged one black shoulder. 'With a bit of luck,' she said, 'something happens to make them grow down again.'

'And without a bit of luck? Do they stay like that till they die?'

'Sure when they're like that, girl, they never really lives. Not properly anyhow. They thinks they knows everything, and sure when you knows everything then you learns nothing. And when you stops learning you're dead, even if you spends the next fifty year running around the place like an eejit. The world is full of dead people, Saskia. Just 'cause they're breathing don't mean they're not dead. They fools other people and they fools themselves, but they can't fool the world. They shuts their eyes to the world, and they shuts their hearts to the world, and that's the true death. People like that are more dead nor the dead.'

'Is Phil a dead person?' Saskia asked.

Birdie had made her sour face. 'Phil is more like someone

walking in his sleep,' she said. 'His eyes is shut, but his heart is open a bit. He was young when his Da died, you know, and it made him very serious. But he's from lively stock, and good blood will tell. All Phil needs is a kick-start, and all this might be just the thing to get him going. Sometimes, Saskia, the best present you can get from life is a good kick. It's never too late, you know. The world is always there waiting. It was there before us all, and it'll stay there after us. And the world is a patient place. There's always a hooley on in the world's house, and there's always a welcome on the mat. And it's never too late to wake up to it.'

'So there's hope for us all then?'

'Yerra, child, sure there's always hope. There's hope for everything.'

'Even Pooshipaws?'

'Oh, aye. Even Pooshipaws.'

'Even Bad Jack Mackey?'

Birdie Murray had looked almost dreamy. 'One day,' she'd said, 'when the world winds itself down a bit, even Jack Mackey will come home.'

Sometimes, when Birdie spoke of Mackey, Saskia sensed an underlying affection beneath the hard words. And even on that frightening night in the old house by the park she had noticed, looking back on it, some echoes of an old friendship between them. Old? It would have to be very ancient indeed. 'When this stone was part of a big rock on a mountaintop,' Birdie had said in that dream by her stream, 'me and Bad Jack Mackey were ould enemies already.'

In bed now, in another country, Saskia was concerned with smaller stretches of time. She looked at her watch. Eleven o'clock – ten in Ireland. She had a hot date tonight – or, to be accurate, a cold one. Simon would be asleep already, and in his sleep she knew he'd be up on an ice-cream mountain with Tiger Mike and the Pooshipaw. Saskia would join them there in a little while, and this time, because she was involved, because she was invited by everyone there, she could really join in. It still wouldn't be as real for her as it was for Simon, because he and the Pooshipaw now were connected in a special way. But it would be pretty good.

Birdie would turn up tonight, in some form or fashion. She and Saskia had arranged it. Saskia knew Birdie was changed now – gone, but not gone. There were no words for what Birdie was; in some ways she was more here than ever. The night would be fun anyway, but Saskia had reasons for wanting to see Birdie, whoever Birdie was now. She'd done all that Birdie had asked; now it was her turn to ask for something.

Saskia suspected that Birdie Murray had known about the Big Idea before it was even clear in Saskia's own head. Though she wasn't sure why or how, Saskia suspected it was part of the reason Birdie had wanted to involve her in this whole business. She'd thought that all Birdie said and did worked on two levels; but the more she thought about it, the more she'd concluded that it was probably closer to forty levels than two. She didn't know how this particular connection worked, but she was sure it was there. Birdie had set all this up.

'It's time you were going,' the old woman had said to her in Mackey's house on Sunday night. Saskia had been in the middle of what seemed like her hundredth question, and hadn't wanted to stop. But Birdie had been very firm.

'It's not done,' she'd said. 'You don't stop a thing till it's done. That's the mistake that Jack makes all the time. And always out of vanity.'

'Are all magicians vain?' Saskia had asked.

'Not all. But all men are, begob. What is done, though, is your part in this thing. You'll go now, and you'll sleep, and in the morning you'll wake up and this will be over.'

'And you? How do you finish these things?'

Birdie had pulled herself erect. She was obviously in some pain, but her eyes flashed and her yellow teeth grinned with real happiness. She held up her two hands in front of her face. Flames blossomed from the tips of her fingers, flames that were more blue and purple than yellow. It looked as though her hands were on fire. Saskia gasped.

'I told you and Simon,' Birdie Murray said, 'that fire is my friend. It does a lovely clean job, fire.'

Smoke came from the ends of her long hair, and little flames started to lick from its edges. Birdie Murray's hair began to stand up on her head, rising as though on a draught of air until it looked like a burning halo standing out from her skull. Saskia looked, hardly recognising the woman she knew in this strange apparition before her. Birdie Murray smiled. She did not seem human any more, but it was hard to say what she was.

Saskia looked down at the old man on the floor. In spite of herself she felt a twinge of pity for him. 'You're going to kill him?' she'd asked.

Birdie Murray laughed. 'Yerra, girl,' she said, 'you don't talk about killing the likes of me and Jack! I'm going to put him out of harm's way for a little while – him and all his works.'

'And then? What will you do then?'

'I'll go home to me bed. And in a little while, I'll have me well-earned rest.'

'Will I see you again?' Saskia asked, wanting terribly to know.

'You will and you won't,' Birdie Murray said, her hands

and her hair blazing now.

'Don't tell me! I'll sort of see you, right?'

Birdie smiled at her with open fondness then. 'In your dreams, girleen,' she said. 'Next week. Sure I owes you a favour. And I pays me debts!'

'Mrs Murray? Birdie?'

'Child?'

Saskia looked at the burning woman, knowing that she was more frightening than Jack Mackey could ever be. 'Mrs Murray,' she said, 'Will you answer me one thing honestly?'

'I will, painter's daughter.'

Saskia had struggled to formulate the question she wanted to ask. 'What *are* you, Mrs Murray?' she asked.

Birdie Murray smiled a buddha-like smile from the flames dancing around her head.

'I'm the sum of the choices I've made,' she said. 'Just like anybody else. But I've lived a long time, *leanaveen*, and so I've made a lot of choices.' She gave a little wave with one flaming hand. 'Goodnight now, *a leana*,' she said.

And the next thing that Saskia knew, she was being woken by the sound of Ruth and Phil's voices in Simon's room, though the heat of the fire had seemed still to be warming her face.

Saskia's dreams now were crazy and colourful things, and she went to bed each night happy. Each night too she was half-afraid that this new thing would fade like the marks on her face, and that she'd be back in her old world of nightly dullness. Simon would never have a problem like this now: the Pooshipaw would take care of that.

It was thinking like this that had given Saskia her Big Idea in the first place. If Pooshipaws made bad dreams, she'd wondered, could they make good ones too? Birdie would know. And Birdie had known – of course.

Saskia crawled under the quilt on the low bed and sighed sleepily. She turned out the light without reading any of her book. What book could compare with the prospect of a night on an ice-cream mountain with a child, a tiger, and a Pooshipaw? Now there was a dream well worth sleeping for, even if it wasn't wholly hers. She was happy, of course, to share it with Simon, though it wasn't even really Simon's dream either. Because the one who made the dream, who planned and executed it, would be the Pooshipaw. Except that now the Pooshipaw didn't come to Simon's dreams as an invader, but as a friend.

Saskia reached under her pillow and held the two small things that lay there – a stone and a bone. She'd found them in her bed on Monday morning, and had clung to them hungrily since. Perhaps their power was gone, but she didn't care: they were her link with her witches and her dreams. The link with the night of the Pooshipaw. At the thought of the monster, she felt the Big Idea grow even more exciting. Because there was more than one Pooshipaw in the world, Birdie had said. Anybody with the knowledge could make a Pooshipaw, and the kind of Pooshipaw they made would depend on the ingredients that they put into it – like a cake. And Birdie knew how to do it.

Saskia lay in the dark and felt a big grin spread slowly across her face. She was very deeply happy. She could feel sleep creeping up on her, and welcomed it. She let it cover her like some slow tide coming in on the beach back home at the bottom of her Irish garden, its waves born off the shores of another continent. She fell asleep smiling and hoping and imagining: smiling at the prospect of her dreams, hoping that Birdie would be there, and imagining – only imagining, mind – a monster of her very own.